WAITING FOR THE
PIANO TUNER TO DIE

WAITING FOR THE
PIANO TUNER TO DIE

HARRIET RICHARDS

THISTLEDOWN PRESS

National Library of Canada Cataloguing in Publication Data

Richards, Harriet, 1953 –
Waiting for the piano tuner to die

ISBN 1-894345-50-9
I. Title.
PS8585.I177W34 2002   C813'.54   C2002-910958-2
PR9199.3.R466W34 2002

Book and cover design by Jackie Forrie
Typeset by Thistledown Press Ltd.
Printed and bound in Canada

Thistledown Press Ltd.
633 Main Street
Saskatoon, Saskatchewan
S7H 0J8

Thistledown Press gratefully acknowledges the financial assistance of the Canada
Council for the Arts, the Saskatchewan Arts Board, and the Government of
Canada through the Book Publishing Industry Development Program for its
publishing program.

for my family, all

ACKNOWLEDGEMENTS

I am grateful to the Saskatchewan Arts Board for their generous support in the writing of this book.

"Requiem", "Andrea's Kitchen", "Spoor", and "Rosa Velos" were previously published in *Planet, the Welsh Internationalist* (Aberystwyth, Wales).

CONTENTS

I CAN'T SEE IT

THEY HAD ALWAYS KEPT CATS, Ed and Alma, as many as could survive without benefit of vets, and when they'd end up with too many, distemper or a mean neighbour would clear them out. Ed would find the corpse sometimes, curled and snarl-mouthed, and dig out a clump of dirt by the caraganas, toss it in and give the turf a thump with the back of the spade. They used to tell Prue the cats had run off, but quit when she was seven or so and had come in crying with the grave-dirt falling from her best kitten, buried too shallow in Ed's hurry, and the red ribbon she'd tied round its neck still fresh and in a bow.

Prue was their only child, and grew up being petted and carried, wrapped and cuddled until she reached an age where she was able to complain about it. Alma had not much experience with children, and saw most things Prue did as appropriate. Prue ate everything on her plate, had friends, and there was never a complaint from any teacher. Prue brought home her best assignments from school and Alma taped them to the cupboards or tacked them on the panelled walls. And when she asked Alma's advice she was generally told: "Well, I don't know the score on that."

Alma ironed absolutely every bit of clothing her daughter wore, even her undershirts and tiny panties, and later on melted a few synthetics whose care tags were faded. As Prue grew up she hid her bras to save them — she'd had to go out and buy those herself — and even the cheap ones weren't cheap.

Every year she got through school, Ed would comment to anybody possible, "Prue's done the sixth grade. She'll be in seven next fall." "Prue's done the ninth grade. She'll be in ten next fall."

They went to the Christmas concerts but not the parent teacher interviews. "Prue never seems no trouble," Alma said, "She's a steady kid."

Prue was done tenth grade, and had decided maybe she would look at beauty school in two years. She spent a lot of time fussing with rollers and spray, and made trips to the city with her friends, returning with cosmetics and lash curlers and hair dyes.

Her parents were shown it all and Alma oh my-ed and chuckled, "We'll have a movie star before the year is out."

It was October when Prue came home from school one morning sick to her stomach; her face was blotchy and mascara had seeped into little black patches on the lids and under the eyes. Alma made some tea, pushed the cats off the couch and settled her on it.

She continued to be sick off and on until mid-November.

Alma said to her, "Prue. Are you sure some boy hasn't been at you?"

Prue mumbled something, closed her thick lids and held her favourite cat to her ribs.

"Oh Prue. You're still a little girl. What in heck's wrong with me, I should've told you about some things."

Prue whispered, "I know about those things. Maybe it's not happening like that."

"Open them eyes and look at your mother. There's my girl. 'Maybe it's not', you said. Has a boy been at you Prue?"

"He said it was safe."

"Did he now. What he are we talking here?"

"Don't matter, Mom."

"It goddammit matters to me."

Prue's eyes stayed open at that one; Alma never swore.

"Just a boy. And he doesn't like me anymore."

"Well no wonder, with you alley-catting. Boys don't respect that."

"Then why'd they do it?"

"Can't help it. It's in their nature. See if they can, and sulk if they can't, and laugh at you if you let them."

"Maybe it's not happening."

Alma sat Prue down to the kitchen table and studied her. The blotches had gone from her face and she'd grown round in the cheeks. She lifted her girl's hand; the fingers were swollen.

"Do you hurt up here?" Alma patted her own chest.

"Just fat. I'm busting out of my bras. Hey, what're you doing?"

Alma rummaged through the lower cupboard and brought out her sewing kit.

"Jesus H. Christ Mom. What are you going to do?"

Alma pulled a yard of black thread from the spool, licked the end and put it through a needle. She was about to knot the ends, but thought differently.

"I'm not going to sew you up, silly. Now lean back and relax, just you close your eyes and don't think about nothing. You're going to be fine."

She knelt by Prue and held her own arm high so the needle dangled like a plumb over Prue's belly. A few seconds went by, and Prue's breathing came long and even. The needle remained still and Alma frowned a little, then gently it began to sway on the thread and she got a look of satisfaction, and watched — while pretending not to watch so the needle wouldn't be aware of her — as it picked up momentum, swaying harder back and forth until suddenly it found the edge of its circle and went round and round, slow and sure.

She smiled. "I've got a granddaughter on the way."

Prue burst into tears.

She did not make it through the eleventh grade.

They had a school meeting with a cheery district guidance counsellor who was determined Prue should stay in school, times had changed, and hold her head high.

"Why the heck shouldn't she hold her head high?" was Alma's retort. "She didn't do this thing to herself you know."

The only problem seemed to be that final exams and the granddaughter's arrival were scheduled to occur at the same time, but Prue became so puffy and ill by April even the guidance counsellor was urging her to go home.

Prue spent the next seven weeks with her feet elevated and various cats kneading the hard belly wall behind which her daughter floated and grew, and when the time came the big German wife of the minister arrived to drive them all into the city.

Ed surprised them by turning off the televison, putting on his hat and pouring tea down the sink.

"This is my goddamned baby too, goddamned women. And that little fucker dairy farmer don't know what he's missing here."

Alma and Prue stopped and stared, wondering just how had he known who it was.

"And I'll be paying that little fucker a fucking visit and just let his fat fucker parents try to shut me down again and I'll have the fucking Mounties throw the whole family in jail."

The minister's wife waited at the doorway, maintaining a tense smile. "Ed, I think we should get this little girl to the hospital."

She drove a Ford Fairlane, wide and comfortable. The moon cast shadows on the fields, so bright they could almost have driven without headlights. Every once in a while, Prue moaned hard.

Alma was proud of the job Prue did; she'd screamed like a fool and then popped out a seven-pound girl in under an hour.

"You mean Rebecca?" they were asked by the nurses.

"Becky is her name, just Becky."

"Should've been a nine pounder," said Alma as she sniffed Becky's scalp, sweet as new jam, "she's so wiry. Likely the swelling on you took a couple pounds off her, Prue."

"Well, that so-called father is a big fucker," muttered Ed. He scrubbed at his nose to stop the tears that had started. "I'm off for some tea. Bring you some Alma, you want."

Prue waited for her father to get well away and down the hall.

"Mom. Maybe it wasn't him."

13

"Don't you tell me this. Don't you tell me this now. If it wasn't him, then who did it to you?"

"Nobody," said Prue.

Alma started to laugh. She laughed so hard she had to hand the baby back to Prue who lay on the hospital bed pale and hollow-eyed and looking like a nine year old.

"Was *not* no *nobody* Prue, unless you just gave birth to the Second Coming. Now look, I can't have Ed making a fool of himself to the wrong boy."

Prue's eyes rolled toward the black window. "He said it was safe."

"Who said? Don't you go silly on me Prue. Was it the dairy farmer kid said so? Was it that Carl or whatever?"

"Yeah."

"Nobody else got at you?"

"Carl never exactly got at me. He said it was safe."

"He doesn't sound too bright. Don't you think about that now. Becky has her little mother and she has me and Ed and she'll be our baby."

Prue figured things would be pretty much the same after all of this. She would play with the baby over the summer and then start grade eleven over again.

The end of August came. She could hardly speak from exhaustion.

Ed, after the first few nights, just roared out in his sleep when Becky cried. Alma and Prue got up together sometimes, or Prue woke her mother if Becky wouldn't settle after a change and bottle. Alma would come out patchy-haired and stooped, to hold Becky as she arched and bucked and screamed and sometimes projected white spew clear across the room. And Alma would walk and croon and finally light a smoke in the middle of the night with the baby laid over her shoulder like a sack of flour, going *oop oop aah, oop oop aah,* dreaming she was still crying.

Ed had his seventy-first birthday the day after Becky slept her first night through. But it was already November and Prue couldn't go back to school.

Becky was early to smile. Even between barfing and screeching those first few months she'd stop and look at the face above her and beam and kick and squeeze her eyes tight with joy. By Christmas she was a full belly-laugher, roaring at everything. She weighed as much as some toddlers, though she wasn't fat, just big and full of life.

Prue had a rickety orange umbrella stroller. One handle slid off all the time when she went in reverse, but she could fold it up and carry it on the bus to the city with Becky and the diaper bag. There she would spend hours in malls, up and down, through the stores, showing off her perfect baby.

At home she was stuck. Ed bought her a short wooden toboggan and she propped Becky all snowsuit and scarf-muffled into a cardboard box and towed her to the store and around the town. But Becky was too hot in the store, and after she'd been presented a few times the girls behind the counter didn't seem as impressed.

Spring came and Ed started getting calls to fix mowers. Their back porch filled with mud as he stomped back and forth from the shed to warm up. Prue fretted over the red stretch marks that hadn't yet faded from her pregnancy, and complained about jeans that stayed too tight. She took up smoking, from boredom, and every day she and Alma rolled up a supply from the tin of Players, filling their plastic cigarette boxes. Her main joy was the monthly baby clinic at the town office, where they dressed Becky in her finest, and brought her to be measured and innoculated, and tested for proper development.

"That Jorgenson kid's an ugly sucker," Alma would declare on the way home, or, "That Miller baby doesn't look right at all, does he Prue?" "That poor little Jessie's going to be a field of freckles like her mother, that woman's darned near an albino, hardly see the lashes on her" "See how Becky spotted them other kids and got all excited, she's a bright one."

Becky grew as she should, all through the year. They tried to keep her from eating too much of the cats' food, and when she learned to walk it was by holding the tip of a cat's tail for balance.

Prue started taking the bus to the city alone.

Ed fixed the stroller handle so his wife wouldn't find it so complicated, and Becky went with her grandmother to whist tournaments and teas, and had a dozen women willing to hold and feed her, or settle her on her blanket or a pile of sweaters, to sleep. Her fuzzy little scalp was growing out and there was much speculation on what kind of hair she'd end up with. Never a mention of paternal influence in these discussions. If any of them knew who'd done it, they didn't mention him in front of Alma.

Prue turned seventeen August 3rd. Alma made her a Devil's Food cake and she and Ed gave her a $25 gift certificate for a teen store in the city, plus a compact assortment of eye shadows, blushes, and brush-on lipsticks.

Prue spent hours doing and re-doing her face and sometimes Becky sat entranced, watching quietly and not grabbing at the brushes, and Prue would give her baby a spot of colour on each cheek, and Becky would put her mouth into a kiss shape so Prue could pretend to give her lipstick.

They would all laugh, Alma too, coughing from it so hard she'd have to give her lungs a spray before declaring, "We've got two movie stars in the house now."

Ed had some success with the dairy farmers, though Prue was adamant she didn't ever want to see that boy again. An envelope with a twenty dollar bill came each month and Prue stuck it in the bank, in trust for Becky.

"Kid's worth more than I am," grumbled Ed.

By the end of the summer Prue had missed the bus back to town four times and had to spend the night with friends.

"School's starting up in a couple of weeks. Ed and I've been talking how we'll miss having you around for the day."

Becky lay sleeping on the corner of the couch, as three cats purred on the edges of her quilt. Prue was doing her makeup, tossing away cotton balls smudged with greens and blues, pinks and blacks, until she got it right. She turned her head left and then right with her eyes straight ahead on herself, and said, "Um."

"What do mean, 'um'? You've got to hustle if you're going to be ready."

Prue looked over at Becky, whose cheeks flushed bright in her snooze and hands curled tight by her head. "She's a good little girl, isn't she?"

"Course. What on earth, Prue, is gotten into you?"

"Um. Thing is, I can't see it going back to school. It's like going to play with a bunch of kids and pretending I'm a kid, and all the intercoms and teachers and doing homework. I just can't see it."

"What *can* you see, Miss Grownup?"

WAITING FOR THE PIANO TUNER TO DIE

"I can see me maybe moving to Red Deer and getting a job."

"You got a job, Prue. Your school and this baby's your job."

Prue sat on the sofa's edge and the cats blinked and stretched at her. "I got a real job if I want it. Guy I know's got a brother with a trucking company and he's got a job there and I got one too if I want. Receptionist and dispatcher-in-training."

Alma lit a smoke and squinted at her, inhaled and blew out hard through the nostrils. She said nothing.

"I get a raise every three months and when I'm full dispatcher a fat one. They got a dental plan and the whole bit."

Ed came in from the porch, dirty boots still on, and sat, knees wide apart, in his chair. He picked up his reading glasses and the *TV Times*. Alma knew he was pretending not to listen. She frowned at his dirt tracks, but stayed silent, pulling on her cigarette and glaring at Prue.

"I can stay with this guy until I get enough saved up and after a while maybe Becky'd come live with me if I can find a babysitter. Stop looking at me. I tell you I just can't see it acting like a kid and going to school. I just can't."

Prue was gone within the week.

When Becky turned three she could hardly quit talking about going to playschool in the fall. The baby fat had left and she was tall for her age, and wiry, and her hair was fluffy and alarmed like the first feathers on a chick. She'd stand on the kitchen chair for Alma to give her plastic dishes to wash and dry, and she'd watch Ed tear apart the

18

mowers and see the blood well up through his black greased fingers, gnarled and thick. When fall came it was Ed who put on his hat and said he'd take the girl to church for her playschool.

Every day she and her grandfather walked hand in hand and down the steps to the church basement and at five to twelve he'd be there to bring her home again.

Alma's asthma had gotten worse and she didn't go out very often, and when she did, Becky was a handful and whined if she was stuck, for instance, at the Senior's hall for the afternoon. Often the little girl was out in the yard or the garage with Ed. He'd give her old tobacco cans and buckets of nails and bolts and screws, and she'd sort them or make little towns with them and fill and empty and rearrange for hours. She'd come inside stained from rust. The cement pad for Ed's welder was covered and recovered with coloured chalk drawings of cats and round-headed families with asterisks for hands, and tic-tac-toes she and Ed fought out while various cats batted their hands or lay beside them in the sun-soaked chalk dust.

When she was about to turn five, Ed and Alma went to the school to preregister Becky for kindergarten. A couple of the young mothers stared pretty hard at them, but the teacher was careful and polite and agreed gravely with all they said: "Yes she is tall for her age, yes I see she knows her colours and letters very well, many children don't, oh she's not quite five? Good for her."

The teacher smiled at Becky who was lining up all of the empty chairs so the legs and seats matched exactly, and smiled at her bare feet in plastic flip-flops that were crushed down and too small, so her heels hung over the backs, and at her thin little face and chipped pink nail polish and mismatched shorts set.

"I think she's a very lucky girl to have grandparents like you."

Alma said to anyone who'd listen, "Becky's five now. She'll be in kindergarten in the fall."

The night before the first day of school Alma ironed everything Becky might want to wear, and next morning let her choose. She wrapped up a cupcake in waxed paper for a snack and Ed put on his hat and walked Becky to the school, hand in hand, past the teenaged smokers and the crowds pushing off the buses, through the door and down the hall to the kindergarten room.

At 11:55 he was waiting outside the classroom door and he walked her home for lunch. He did that the entire year.

The kindergarten teacher phoned them just once, stuttering and apologetic. Becky had used the "f" word.

Ed and Alma sat her down and gave her a bowl of Cheerios before bed.

Alma said, "Your teacher was mad at you and she called."

"Goddammit woman shut the hell up. Listen Becky, you can't say fuck at school. That's it. They don't like it when people say fuck at school. Nobody's mad at you. Your teacher says you're the best kid there."

"Okay," said Becky, and dug into the Cheerios, milk dripping on her chin. "I don't *have* to say it."

The fall Becky was in second grade, she told Ed that if he left her on the corner across from the school she could walk the rest of the way by herself. He waited there at noon and again at 3:30, listening for the bell, leaning on the big elm, hands in pockets, watching for her or the purple hat which might give her away at a distance.

Their kitchen cupboard doors were papered with scotch-taped layers of school art and printing assignments.

It was April, Becky's third grade, when Prue phoned squeaking and loud. "It's a June wedding."

Alma wondered, only a second, where it would be and who had to pay. For that entire second, she had a vision of Prue extravagant in lace and veils, and of them all at the United Church which was filled, and a buffet waiting at the Elk's Hall, helium balloons and a wedding dance. She covered the phone to cough, and then spit into her wadded up hanky.

"Who the heck are you marrying, Prue?" At least it wouldn't be the trucker, or the CN guy, likely not any of them she'd phoned about.

"What do you mean who the heck? Alex. Took him long enough, almost a year. Are you getting weird Mom? Alex, the nice one. Teaches at the business college. Mom, Mom, Becky's getting married too. He wants lots of kids and he wants Becky."

"Tell him he can't have her. What kind of nerve is that? She isn't his. A man just can't come from nowhere and say the word and steal a kid from her home. What kind of . . . I don't know."

"She's *my* kid." Prue said it nastily.

Alma listened to the crackle of ash from her cigarette and Prue's shaky breath coming too loud through the receiver over a background of street noise.

"Course she's your kid. And she's mine and Ed's too."

"She is *my* kid. And me and Becky are going to buy a new house with Alex in Red Deer. She can go to movies and play in the park and have a dishwasher and a car."

"She's only eight, Prue. She can't drive." It was a stupid thing to say, she knew it was, but everything had become stupid.

Prue forced her voice level. "I appreciate everything you did for her. You and Dad. Don't think I don't appreciate everything you did for her."

Words screamed in Alma. There were things she needed to explain but shouldn't even have to explain, they were so clear. She wanted to say: you don't appreciate *shit*, Prue. You don't have a clue. You never were too bright, you got by. Not like Becky, she's bright as the morning sun. You take her away from here and you wouldn't know what to do with her and you wouldn't know who she is and she sure as heck wouldn't know what to make of you.

Alma managed to say, "I don't think it's right," but started coughing so badly she put the phone down and bent double. Her smoke fell, still lit, on the linoleum. When she was able she retrieved it, and crushed it into the ashtray. There was a brown scorch mark on the floor. She grabbed the puffer and used it twice, head hurting and dizzy, and cursed herself until she could speak again.

She went back to the phone. Prue had hung up.

Next time she talked to her daughter, it was in person, and Prue was very quiet. Alex was with her, so round-headed he reminded Alma of Becky's pre-school drawings. They had driven from Red Deer and just shown up and would spend the night in the city. But Alex insisted they stop first, saying he couldn't wait to meet them all.

Ed was silent for most of the visit, and snubbed Alex's hearty attempts to get him talking about his workshop, or the weather, or this great little town. He left for the shed at one point — to work, he'd said — and came back twenty minutes later to find Becky showing Alex her toys: a broken Mousetrap game from the rummage sale, a Cabbage Patch baby, several Barbies and a stuffed elephant.

"This has been great, thanks so much. We'll come by after lunch tomorrow and fill each other in some more."

Ed spoke. "Listen you little fucker. Becky lives here and that's it."

Prue rolled her eyes and said to Alex, "Didn't I just tell you?"

She believed she'd never been more ashamed of her parents. Her mother with orange-stained fingers and wearing a cat-snagged knit top over some other woman's out-of-date slacks. And her crazy, pale-eyed fool father almost eighty years old, standing there like he thought he was in charge of the world.

Alex smiled politely at Ed and turned to Alma. "One step at a time they say. Let's not rush each other."

Alma didn't answer, and she lay awake half the night.

Next day Prue barged past Alex into the front room. There was an ugly look to her.

"Where's Becky?"

Alma was cutting her toenails, one foot up on the coffee table. She brushed the clippings into her palm and set them in the ashtray.

"Why, she's off with her friends somewhere. It *is* Saturday. I'll make some tea."

Alex said, "That would be nice."

"You could've at least made her stay home to see her own mother." Prue's voice grew hard and whining. "Maybe she doesn't want to see me anymore, is that what's going on here? You telling her all the time what a bad mother I am?"

"I never did Prue."

"I've done nothing wrong. I was just a little girl and you damn well know that. Just a little girl and I had to go out and work for a living and now things are going good and I'm ready to take my baby back. And you should be thanking me." She'd gone pasty and her hands and head trembled as she knocked a cigarette out from Alma's pack.

Alex jumped up and took it from her.

"Jesus, Alex. I'm not starting up again. I just can't see it going through this without a smoke."

He gave it back and sat down.

Alma thought she should say something friendly, or settling. "Well now. When's the big day, Alex?"

"June 26th, Grace Church, and reception at the hall there. Won't be a big affair, we've got to count our pennies. You and Ed can stay at a motel, our treat."

"Oh. Isn't that nice."

Everything about this was starting to make her sick, the least of which was finding a way to pay for a trip to Red Deer.

Alex cleared his throat and shuffled himself closer to the edge of his chair. Alma could easily imagine him turning to fat within a few years.

Prue took a last, long drag and tapped out her cigarette on the nail clippings. There was a brief smell of burning hair. They both faced Alma.

Alex reached, as if he was about to take Alma's hand, but she quickly grabbed her mug of tea and tilted it up to drink. It was empty, but maybe they hadn't noticed.

He said, "Now listen Mrs., uh, can I call you Mom?"

"You can call me Alma."

"Alma, this is not an easy situation. I know how attached you — and your husband too, I guess — must be. And it will certainly be an adjustment for us all. Haha, me included. I'm sure there will be some bumps along the way, so my friends with kids tell me."

Alma had to say something here. She said, "What are you talking about?"

Prue hissed and rolled her eyes.

Alex looked over at her, puzzled, then back to Alma. This time he spoke very gently. "We're talking about Becky."

"I thought we cleared that up last night. I'd say Ed told it pretty straight to you last night." Her voice sounded peculiar to herself, as if it came from somewhere or somebody else.

"He said some things, but I'll put it down to shock. I'm sure he'll come round soon enough. Now Prue here had wanted lawyers to be in on this. She figured things might not be clear and she was all for getting a lawyer to talk to you. And I said, no, let's just visit them and everything will work out in a natural way. Isn't that what I said, Prue?"

"Something like that." Prue lit another of her mother's cigarettes and stared at her feet. It was a miracle, she thought, that she'd gotten out of this place when she did.

She watched her feet for a long time.

ROSA VELOS

HER NAME IS ROSA VELOS AND SHE IS FOUR YEARS OLD. She has on yellow corduroy long pants and leather Buster Browns which her mother has carefully double-tied for her, and a zippered wool cardigan with a black poodle in relief on each of its front pockets.

She is running fast, and as she runs she stretches out her arms to flail the tall grasses and the burdock and the milkweed as she goes through them. Everything is tall but herself. The white goat which her father declared to be a hermaphrodite, and Rosa named Sally, follows her now, but the milking nanny, although playful, stays in the yard. Also running with her is their border collie Muff, who mostly lopes in great circles around them or streaks after birds or the small animals only he can see.

She stops to reach up for the bristly pod of a milkweed so she can squeeze out the thick white syrup for a taste which now she doesn't know for sure is sweet or bitter. When she stops she also sees the bruised face of the moon which is risen pale against the mid-afternoon sky.

Muff is maybe chasing a vole or deer mouse, and whenever he catches one he always comes back and shows her, grinning, with the mouse's tiny paws and tail hanging from between his tightly clamped jaws. And he holds it there a while, she believes, as she herself would a cinnamon heart, to melt its hard, sweet surface and make the rest more chewy. Her socks are coated in itchy little burrs which she picks off far slower than they reappear. It is very possible the hermaphrodite Sally is not there for this run, how could she be? She should have to be tied to her rope or safe in the pen, but Rosa still remembers her jumping lightly through the timothy and nettle and milkweed toward the ravine, calling out her wobbly *wa-aa, wa-aa,* as young goats do. Rosa picks a couple of sprigs for the kitchen table — hairy-stemmed bright-blues, which her mother calls blue devil. She drops them, she forgets where, before she gets home.

One day Rosa finds herself sitting on the lino floor of their living room playing paper dolls with another little girl. They use short snub-nosed scissors to cut around the paper tabs of crinolines and little paper purses that always fall off the dolls themselves which are made of a heavier stock. This other girl is strange to Rosa for many reasons. She is dark haired, as is Rosa, but with a dusty kind of skin, and her fingers leave greasy smudges on Rosa's carefully coloured paper doll party dresses. Her shoes are black patent leather, but cracked and scuffed, and dirty pink socks bulge around their straps. What is oddest of all to Rosa, is this girl's smell. Salt fish, garlic, and something else — a cellar smell.

What's your name? asks Rosa over and over that day. In answer, the girl sometimes says a word under her breath, or looks to her right or left and makes a kind of whistling

WAITING FOR THE PIANO TUNER TO DIE

sound. *What's your name?* over and over. After they become friends this becomes a joke: *What's my name?* Emily asks and they laugh and Rosa will answer Sally, billygoat, Muff, my clown-doll, Mrs. Shoes.

Does Emily's mother bring her for the visit that first day?

Rosa thinks she sees Emily's mother once, shadowy and bulky through the screen door into Emily's kitchen and cabbage-smell steaming out to the yard where they've run back to use the outhouse.

But Rosa's mother says Emily's mother is gone. Has she once been there and then left?

It is some time during this autumn that Emily also begins to run with Rosa, and they run together for almost four years.

Rosa doesn't know exactly when the rats begin to invade her sleep. But it seems her terror has been there for a long time before it possesses a form and a name, and she is able to tell her mother what wakes her sobbing in the middle of the night. Her mother finally offers Rosa five cents for every nightmare she doesn't have. Rosa does not recall ever collecting a single nickel.

The rats she finds in her sleep are of an evil so suffocating that she believes, every time, she will very probably die.

She isn't certain from where came the word itself: *evil.* And it is not until many years later she realizes with surprise that she has used the word in prayer since first memory. *Lead us not into temptation but deliver us from evil.* The evil in prayer seems a very different word, one that covers problems like stealing pennies or cookies. Rosa's evil is of the sort easily recognised by a very little girl, one who knows it without being told.

She has two separate dreams, both of them over and over, and in one of these she experiences the same scene as if it has never happened before, and so each time comes close to dying from it.

This is the scene she doesn't die through over and over: It is sunny in her bedroom. There is her bed and the varnished headboard with decals of a skipping bear holding a picnic basket, and a fat bluebird over the bear's shoulder. The sun streams through the open window and she can hear her mother and father talking together quietly downstairs and sometimes the goats and Muff and the chickens far away outside. She is standing and looking at her bedroom before she is forced to turn and go into the closet. The closet has one light bulb and a long string attached to the chain which will turn it on. She knows that the light never goes on. There is no refuge in a dark closet, and the door to the hall is all the way across the floor. She takes a step. The room is silent now, thick with sunlight and her fear. Only a few steps to reach the door, but as always she must stand very still and quiet and wait. The two rats come out from under her bed, black and shiny as seals, ducking and bending as humans would, walking upright. Their eyes are red, and they are smiling at Rosa, never speaking. Their hissing breath comes to her before they are fully out. They walk toward her on their padded black feet and she begins to die.

As is the way with dreams she tries to scream for her parents but there is nothing left in her but one choking intake of breath.

The other rat, there is just one, is much different. When she finds him in her sleep, over and over, Rosa always wonders how it is possible that she is the only one to know who he is, and why he is there. He stands quietly, tall as a man, with his back to the wall deep inside a shed, a shed filled with boxes and crates and old harness and hemp ropes. She goes into the shed to look for something, even though it is not her shed, and walks back and back toward him through squinting sunbeams that pierce the rough-cut splintered walls.

Rosa Velos runs with Muff and now, most times, with Emily. Sometimes Emily seems more of an animal than does Muff or Sally, the gentle hermaphrodite goat. Emily almost always wears dirty dresses and her cracked patent leather shoes which have no purchase on the slippery rocks and grassy banks of the ravine. She seems more like something that has been disguised as a little girl, and later on there are times when Rosa says she hates her, but doesn't know why she would tell Emily such a lie. Emily's shins are bruised and scraped and her dark skin is often pink-blotched from scab picking. She does a thing which reminds Rosa of Muff when he stops to growl at a distant threat: Emily smiles with her teeth showing and she stares far off at nothing Rosa can see, and she makes a sound that should be a laugh but is more as if she says *ha ha ha* at the back of her throat. Very often after this she thrusts her arms wide like wings and spins for a while, and when she stops, she seems better.

When Emily sees Muff with a mouse's tail and little paw coming out from between his lips, she is delighted and says let's catch a mouse. Rosa has never considered the possibility of this but they go to the old horse barn at Emily's place. Right away Emily has pushed over a matted layer of straw to show Rosa. There are little pink slugs, blind and curled-up and bald, and Rosa says what are they? and Emily says what you never saw baby mouses before let's kill them. They are so ugly and small, but Rosa can seen how pretty they will become after fur and tails grow and eyes are opened. They could be pets, she could take them home with her.

But Emily picks up a mouse between her thumb and pointed finger, her hand delicate, and rolls its head as she would an eraser on the end of a pencil until it pops. She sighs and her teeth show in a thin smile and her eyes are closed like the mouse's until she opens them to drop the mess and wipe her hand on the straw, then on her skirt. You try she says. Rosa wants to cry, but giggles instead, and then has to run home and pee.

Now when Rosa wakes in the morning, her sheets and nightie are soaked and once again her mother offers her five cents, this time for every dry bed. Plastic wrap goes over her mattress and if her morning bath is too fast, at times she can smell on her own arms and legs the same musty odours which she now recognises as part of Emily's.

Emily sometimes finds things that Rosa doesn't. She finds the nest with three eggs and one dead baby bird that had bits of shell stuck to it, but she doesn't say let's kill them, she says let's see what happens if we drop this egg. Rosa drops the first one and a grey-blue featherless chick appears. Emily drops the other two, and afterwards they spend a long time pulling the shell and gummy stuff away from the birds, using twigs. Everything smells so bad that

Emily finally stomps on one of the chicks, leaving it like a tiny wrinkled bag on the ground. Rosa says lets bury them and they do, except for the one Emily squashed.

The earth accepts and cleans such things, not like skin, skin saves smells as if they were stains.

When Rosa plays in the dirt, she sees how it is made of so many grains loosened by hundreds of secretive insects and by the grassy fine roots; the soft earth welcomes it all, the shit and the dead, the pellets of goats, the squashed and eyeless fledgling which has come apart so gradually each day she and Emily check on it. How human-like are these newly formed animals, the mice and birds, hairless and featherless and easily killed.

She remembers Emily being pulled up from the well, although Rosa's mother becomes enraged and slaps her when Rosa speaks of this and says that Rosa absolutely was nowhere near the event. Rosa says the maple sugar horse had a rope tied to it and the end was tied to Emily and there was a pulley for the bucket but it was Emily the horse drew from the well; Emily, folded over limp and dripping with her socks and shoes left at the bottom of the well.

Rosa thinks Emily washed herself clean in that well, which is why she came to be there. She bobbed around scrubbing away the scabs and the pee smell, the sour mushroomy smell, the dark, yellowing blotches that Rosa could often see under the puffy short sleeves of Emily's dress or on her legs. She scrubbed the black spots on her teeth and pulled off each cracked shoe by its heel using the toes of the other foot and peeled her pink socks away and wriggled her feet in that clean black water. Rosa knows how the dirt from Emily's plaid dress would slowly come loose and wander away from her and off into the water like rivulets of smoke; and when Emily was clean and her shoes were lost she would be too tired maybe to climb up the sides and she would go to sleep and then drown. She is glad that Emily was not left there in the wet. Rosa likes to think of her in the ground, although she gets a slap for saying that to her mother. Rosa cannot say it any other way, and is burning hurt that her mother thinks it is so bad of her. But it is true. Emily is to be put in the ground, as well as going to heaven of course, and Rosa says the ground is a good place for her.

Rosa hears them all talking after Emily is found. Is she at home or Emily's? She can hear the voice of Emily's father, though he has no face, but she knows it is him. He says many times, *that little girl was a saint she was my helper she prayed every night before bed God bless mommy and daddy and if I die before I wake I pray the Lord my soul to take she was a saint.* Each time he says it other people agree with him and cry, and say *God rest her only the good die young.*

Rosa wonders at him speaking this way. She never hears him speak like that; she only knows what Emily's father sounds like when he breathes.

Rosa's mother and father talk to her first. They say something very sad has happened and Emily has gone to heaven. But they seem angry with Rosa somehow. She hears them talking between themselves and to Emily's father and on the telephone.

Once, a huge policeman sits in the living room with Rosa and her parents and asks how many times she and Emily have taken the lid off that well to put things there, but Rosa says *we never did.* She thinks, even if we took that big lid off Emily didn't have to go in there unless she wanted. She wonders if she and Emily ever did drop something in the well. They throw things into the old dugout and into the ravine, so maybe they did. She says to the policeman, *maybe we did*. Rosa goes with her mother and father in the pickup and the policeman drives in his car. Rosa's mother is crying. Rosa falls asleep and her father wakes her when they get to Emily's. Why are they there? Rosa hates this place. The house she has never entered, the spidery outhouse, the smelly shacks and horse barn, everywhere rusty wheels and bits of machines choking in yellowed grass. The policeman says to show him how she and Emily put things into the well. Rosa says okay, is that the well? She has to make sure since everyone is staring at her. Rosa says where is the lid? and the policeman shows her and Rosa says, no the big lid. But it isn't there. Instead there is a round plank of wood on the round top of the corrugated steel wall, but Rosa can't even budge that and catches the tips of her fingers on it, leaving them scratched and filled with splinters. The policeman says is this the lid you and Emily played with? Rosa says no, it was the big lid but it was too big and so is this one.

Rosa's mother scolds her for lying to Emily's father about playing with the well, and that Emily's father had even believed it.

Rosa wonders when Emily's father would ever have heard that she played with the well because she just said it today.

BOY PASSES TURTLE

WILLIAM WAS NOT QUITE SIX YEARS OLD when he decided he was a very happy person. He never strayed from that opinion, and he thought back to the moment of his decision many times.

There had been nothing unusual about the day. He found himself occupied in a fairly ordinary way, kneeling on one of the dining room chairs in order to reach the table and the picture he was colouring. He had made several whales, black and shiny with the crayon's wax, and each with a big white eye on the side of its head; and above them a little house with three windows and smoke curling from a chimney, a fat brown tree beside it with red dots — for birds — in the branches and smaller green dots, for leaves. The surface of the ocean water was a string of turquoise blue "u"s across the paper, and the house and tree rested in the white space above, which was the land, although he hadn't seen a need to define the division with crayons. As he worked, William had the kind of thoughts that are the equivalent to humming: *Whales do swim and trees are rooted in the earth beside houses where small boys live with their mothers and get sore knees from kneeling on the seats of chairs in order to sit high enough to make pictures at the table.*

WAITING FOR THE PIANO TUNER TO DIE

The day had been tired and soft and overcast, a bit bored like himself before his mother got the drawing things out, and as he made just one last red bird he realized there was no sun in his picture. He could use crayon and layer the wax to make the sun thick like the whales' skin, or fill the sun with a yellow felt pen, but that had a lemony ink and part of the tip was wrecked from running it over blue which hadn't completely dried, so sometimes dirty streaks showed up where they didn't belong. He decided on the crayon and put the sun in its corner, high and round and golden as it should be, then sat back because his right knee was aching. As he rubbed the red and wrinkles away from his skin, the real sun came out fast from its break in the clouds and shone through the window's tangle of ivy and wandering jew, scattering tiny pale shadows onto the house, the bird-filled tree and the whales. Everything, every image on the paper's surface seemed to shift and sparkle. He became consumed with awe for a sun that could cause the subtle dancing of whales and houses, and for those whales and houses which allowed themselves to be danced, and understood that a very special thing was happening. William was filled with that wonder, and that was the moment he knew everything would always be all right because he was such a happy person.

Even as he found himself dying, several years later and also on an afternoon, his conviction in this was firm.

William lived by himself with his mother, Steph, who was auburn-haired, small in the hip, and shorter than William by the time he turned twelve. They shared their house with an insane white cat named Tistou, who broke out of curled-up sleeps to leap at ghosts, startling neighbours or the occasional salesman. A few of those neighbours believed Steph to be French, but there was no such thing in her family which Nana, Steph's mother, had traced through five generations in the USA, back to the Midlands of England. Whenever Steph spoke of this, William pictured a green and quiet place, in spirit not much removed from where they now lived, but without the winter. The people there lived in small stone houses and burned peat to cook lamb stew in cauldrons. The Midlands was the place that everyone else passed through, or went around, on their way to more interesting or dangerous lands, toward bogs and mountains, castle keeps, hags in caves, villages bothered by wyverns and bandits.

Sometimes his Nana came for short visits, but not very often because it was very expensive to fly to the prairies from Arizona.

It was Nana who claimed she read the article about a boy who passed a turtle.

It was Steph who claimed Nana had read this to her once over the phone, but Nana had no recollection of doing that. Neither of them could exactly recall the article itself, or why the event had made the Tucson newspaper.

Driving down the highway sometimes his mother would floor their '78 Volare and yell "Lady Passes Turtle", or "Lady Passes Geriatric Turtle".

At age six, William had never seen a turtle, although he searched the ditches and the edges of sloughs near town, and poked around the spring puddles and tall grass in empty lots where he found only toads and grasshoppers and crickets. And one time, at dusk, near summer's end, he and his mother were walking along the outskirts of town. A small animal rushed across the road in front of them, then froze in the streetlight's pool as they approached. It was a salamander, about six inches long. As they leaned over it, the tail suddenly curved up hard toward its head and it became a huge scorpion, feet tight together and now poisoned tail ready to attack. Steph gasped and her hand had instinctively gone out flat in front of his chest to hold him back, and they stood for minutes while the salamander stayed stiff and menacing. Finally they backed off quietly, toward the corner and away from the light, then watched during the split second the salamander took to become amphibious once more and rush into the grass at the street's edge.

Steph bombarded Will with questions the whole way home, and then these became their questions to be passed back and forth a long time afterward: *How could it know a way to become a scorpion? How would a prairie mud puppy have any notion of a nasty desert beast? Why would it understand people are frightened of scorpions?*

Will *did* know what his mother would have done had it attacked them. She would kill it fast, even if it stung her first and she was dying; she would kill it and then possibly throw up because he'd seen her do that once when she'd tried to trap a mouse in a pail and accidentally broken its head or neck. Blood was coming from one of its eyes, and she buried the mouse behind the compost, came back inside and threw up. But still, she would have killed a scorpion.

She was, he knew even then, a fierce sort of mother and he'd witnessed a few times the terrifying, protective force in her. Once they were walking along the gravelled road up toward the old highway when a pickup truck passed them hard on the right, the driver glimpsed by William as lean and teenaged and bent over the wheel. The truck stopped at the sign, roaring, with the box heaving and rocking as the guy gunned the accelerator in neutral, then let go. The rear tires dug into the soft gravel and he heard thunder in the spray of dust and rocks thrown back at him, stinging his arms and legs, smacking so hard his head hurt and he sat in the middle of the road.

Steph tore after the truck. He could hear the sobs in her screaming words: *You little shit get the hell back here right now you little bastard.*

William felt the dribble of blood start to run down his forehead and across one eyelid, and he lowered his face so the drops splashed silently, turning black in the dust on the road. His mother came toward him, teeth clenched, red in the face, skinny in her jeans and sleeveless denim top.

She hugged him up into her, chanting, "He could have blinded you. He could have killed you."

"My head hurts," said Will.

His mother started to cry, softly and angrily, but quit almost as soon as she started. She knelt down with him and held him at arm's-length, and made him follow her finger as she drew a slow line back and forth in front of his face, then made him count backwards from twenty, and then stared into each of his eyes.

"I'll buy you a fudgesicle," was what she finally told him.

He grew up with her saying: Be polite, don't make fun of people, share, give, forgive. But he knew if the right button got pushed it was every man for himself, run for cover and call the exorcist.

She'd brought the local Mountie in for the gravel spewing episode, and this is what William heard her report to his Nana, the old couple next door, the women at the Co-op and the guy who ran the service station: "The Mountie said if I had called him the week before he would have said 'no big deal', but he said same thing happened couple nights ago and shattered the windshield on the patrol car." And then his mother would say, "People used to be *killed* by stoning, why would this jerk need any more proof than that?"

William could have been killed. The thought made him happy all over again.

According to his Nana, he could have died when he was born because he was so little, and was the size and colour of a shaved muskrat. He'd had big purplish-lidded eyes that looked straight out at everyone in the delivery room, as if he'd already been in the world for quite a while.

When William was ten years old he formally met the most beautiful girl in their town. She lived only a block away, and he was not yet in love with her.

Annette, the most beautiful girl, also lived alone with her mother, in a tiny house across the street and down the block from William. She was starting kindergarten when he was trying to quit diapers, which put her a few years ahead of him.

When their formal meeting occurred she was thirteen years old and completely smooth all over, sun-browned and straight legged and, he thought, extremely pleasant and amazing to look at. He knew it was a funny observation, especially as he was once again in pain and sitting in the middle of the street. But she was so balanced and strong and glorious standing and frowning over him as she did, putting her foot out to stop the spinning tire of his red BMX.

She said, "I see you're wearing your crash helmet. So why are you crying?"

"I don't think I'm crying."

"Yes you are. I'm Annette. I know you, you know. You're William right?"

He nodded and, surreptitiously he hoped, wiped his nose on a shoulder.

"And I bet you anything your mother got you that helmet and made you wear it."

"She never made me."

"Okay. She never made you. You've got it on all wrong, it's supposed to sit flat so you don't knock the brains out of your forehead."

"My head isn't what hurts." He turned to one side and pushed up the leg of his knee-length shorts to show off a huge red scrape, streaked with blood and gravel.

She winced and said, "Sorry I bugged you. Want me to take you home?"

"That's a completely alarming thought." He burned deep as the words came out of his mouth. What a stupid, maybe insulting thing to tell her, what an ignorant word: *alarming*; it was as if his mother had taken control of his voice. It was Steph he was alarmed about — probably in the kitchen chopping vegetables and listening to loud Motown, their house filled with posters and tacked up pictures cut from *Rolling Stone* and *Vogue*, and Annette would see it all and be hugged for saving William, and Steph would decree knee and elbow pads from then on.

But Annette laughed, and picked up his bike. "Okay. I wouldn't want to *alarm* you, couldn't have that."

41

"I'm not alarmed." Things were getting worse by the word.

She laughed really hard at that. "You don't look alarmed, this is not very alarming and I don't hear any alarms. How's your knee, going to be okay?"

"Sure. Thanks."

"You're welcome."

He hopped back on the BMX, pretended to rev the handle grips and as he swung around Annette, he couldn't help himself. He yelled, "Boy passes turtle."

She would despise him, how could she not? But afterwards, all the rest of that year, when she met him in the hall at school she grinned and nudged him and said, "Hi, bike-man."

The image of her dazzled all over his head. She was so perfect, like a doll, but no doll any girl he knew had ever owned, maybe a girl who dolls are copied from, maybe that's why guys in old movies said "what a doll" and "doll-face" and "who's the doll?" Because Annette had china blue eyes and roses in her lips and cheeks, and teeth that sparkled, and her skin was not pink or brown, but some soft colour that had no name.

At the time he met the most beautiful girl, he was already in love with someone else, a dark-eyed tomboy who'd just moved into his class, a smiling, straight A's, hockey-playing person named Mandy. She sat three rows from himself, three desks from the front, arriving the third day of school, the numerical coincidence of which was a definite omen as far as William was concerned. He continued to love her for the next few years, a love that drove him almost mute in her presence. She was kind to everybody, and all words and gestures of friendship coming his way were suspect because of it; there was no way of knowing how she might really feel about him. Even so, he wrote notes to her which were never sent and formed a thin, definite bulk under his mattress.

When he got pneumonia and was carrying a high fever Mandy sent him a handmade card from school. It arrived, complete with Star Wars stickers and balloons coming out the mouths of Obi Wan and Chewbacca with Mandy's writing, "To a good friend", "Please get better".

On a Thursday, when he had recovered enough to get back to class, he saw her just one last time. Mandy smiled as she told him her family was moving on the weekend, and William sat through the afternoon dazed and angry. His teacher gave him a note for his mother which read, "William does not seem at all well, maybe consider keeping him home a little longer."

Steph made him stay in his room for the entire Friday, where his crying forced a return of the fever. The next morning he rooted around for the sharp paring knife he'd borrowed from the kitchen months earlier, with a hieroglyphic warrior stamped on the blade. He might take that knife and plant himself on the solid line of the highway in front of town, and stop Mandy's family in their loaded mini-van. But he didn't.

She was gone, and in his pain he found himself in an unfamiliar, deeply private place.

On Sunday, Steph looked at him and said, "I hear Mandy's gone, I bet you're going to miss her."

That was the awful thing about his mother, firstly how she would even know about his passion, and then have the nerve to comment on it, not understanding how deep it cut.

Then she said, "Listen kid, life might swallow you completely and forget to shit you out for a few years, but never, *never* let it take control."

By this, he understood that Life will, eventually, pass person.

William had never thought it was necessary to fear much of anything, mainly because his mother did enough of that for them both. In fact he believed the fears he did have were so insignificant and silly he rarely confided them to Steph, and some he didn't have the heart to because they were mostly risen from the books she read to him.

She read to him every night, and if he was sick and asked, then too. He usually didn't interrupt her if a word was strange, a word like that would just slide into the waves of a story, but if someone was doing something that didn't make sense, he'd say *stop*, and they would talk about it. She read Tolkien and C.S. Lewis and George A. MacDonald. And before that were meticulously illustrated books, with disturbing images of numbats and glow-fishes and tigers on their hind legs, robbers with knives clenched in their teeth, cobras in sluices (*what were sluices?*) coiled and waiting to kill children as they slept.

The Fox was the name he'd given his only serious fear, without knowing, even as he grew older, why it was called this. The Fox was the dark thing that flitted around the edge of his room sometimes, not quite vanishing when he tried to trap it in his sights. He would suddenly feel its eyes on his back when all the lights were on, pencil crayons scattered by his drawing as he knelt on the floor, TV noise pulsing from downstairs — and he would sit up, carefully and deliberately with the hairs stiffening on his arms and a cold pain at the back of his neck. First he would gently push away the pad of drawing paper, raise a knee so one foot was solid and braced, clutch two of the longest pencils dagger-style, then whirl around and search. He'd search that room inch by inch, but always the Fox had known he was armed and was long gone. The paring knife seemed to keep it away for a while, but when William next felt its presence he was sure he could hear it laughing. It quit when he grabbed a pencil. *What if he didn't have pencils?*

And it was the Fox who somehow held the secrets of those other creatures, not exactly ruling them, but leading them out from the subterranean rivers where they were born, and into William's books; making its own journey toward his bedroom through caverns mazed with mineral icicles, swimming past the blind fish, slipping up through the soil with less substance than mist.

There were definite rules, he believed, that Horrors lived by. William trusted those rules more than the ones given out by the usual arbiters, teachers for instance, or the imperious girls in his class.

The first evening he was old enough to be left alone, he indulged in some of the small crimes he had planned: eating too much ice cream, sorting through Steph's jewellery box without permission, making six pieces of toast and peanut butter, and finally going to the basement to test the pail of purple wine, which hadn't yet been siphoned into the carboy and still burped a yeasty vinegar. In the damp of the basement he found, next to the carboy, one of those tiny crab-like spiders he and Steph hated, black and seed-shaped, walking sideways and snapping its pincers. This was not a spider he believed ever built a sunlit

45

web or ate flies, but was an evil, hybrid creature, and William crushed it twice before it quit wiggling. A tremor coursed back and forth between his tailbone and the soles of his feet, and he forced himself not to run, but to be casual as he went up the stairs and to not, no matter what, look behind. From the kitchen he called his friend Adam, who said he'd be right over with some video games. The Fox was out of luck.

William had no intention of growing up, because by doing so he would jeopardise being happy. Even at age fifteen he could sometimes be found riding around town on his bike carrying his air rifle, peering as if blind through thick-lensed glasses he'd bought a joke shop, and in the stupidest clothes possible — such as loud madras shirts and wool trousers yanked way past his waist. In this disguise he would act simple-minded around some of the older people, whom he knew were never quite sure it was William, and he'd yell out *hi there mister* or *halt, you're busted.* His friends, and even Steph, thought these routines were pretty funny. He was doing this while the most beautiful girl was in her third year of going out with Ron.

The girls at school compared Ron to movie actors they thought were hot at the time. With his athletic build and black features — heavy brows, thick lashes over dark blue eyes — and long, expressive hands, he drew attention to himself on and off stage. The senior plays were chosen with him in mind by the adoring drama teacher. William believed him to be a creep. Ron's lips were one giveaway, being pouty and almost girlish, often going to red, but the real reason was William had never seen Ron be a human being to anybody who couldn't actually serve him somehow. William believed himself to be a handsome boy, but he didn't let that interfere with being a human being, and he didn't let being human interfere with having a good time.

It was during one of these bike excursions, and the only time he even slightly hesitated in his chosen route, that he saw Annette and Ron walking hand in hand toward him. They walked as lovers do, with Annette swinging around in front of Ron and folding herself backwards into him as they drew closer to William. Ron with the sneering face, allowing himself a small smirk in response to Annette's laughter and William balanced on his bike, moving slowly as possible without falling over as he watched them. Ron's eyes caught his and moved away, but Annette took in William's rifle and silly clothes and grinned as she yelled a "Hi" to him.

He gave her the thumbs up and then circled the pair once, carefully, forcing them to stop on the road, smiling back at Annette while Ron rolled his eyes and whispered, "What is *up* with this freak?"

Annette's mother had married, and left Annette their tiny house, which she soon shared with Ron. He lasted a year of university before leaving to an acting school in Toronto and from there, it was predicted, on to Stratford and movies, or something equally famous.

Several times Ron returned to Annette. The first time, Steph informed William that there were rumours of marriage. But Ron was offered, and took, a minor role in an American soap. After his character was killed off halfway through the season, he came back to town once more, settled in with Annette and told anyone who asked that he was on a hiatus from acting, and was now writing.

Meanwhile, William's bike, or at least the adventuring aspect of it, had been supplanted by an old Volvo Sedan which he drove like a Ferrari down back roads, across the snaking creek over and over, only slowing for panicked goslings who chirruped behind fat mothers, or cattle being moved to pasture. He patched up rust, replaced brake pads and the front end, kept it waxed and tuned and wouldn't let his friends smoke in it.

Steph liked to say: "If that car was a woman, I'd be a grandmother."

William liked to say that his life was now his own.

It was this position — eighteen years old and life truly being his own — that he toasted at his after-grad party, so it should not have surprised him as it did, after many toasts, when he noticed Annette sitting by herself near a bonfire. She looked lost, or maybe a little embarrassed, although there were others from her old class dancing and loud, up by the deejay. Surprised or not, he knew it was the exact time for a rescue.

"Hi," she said.

William said, "I find myself pissèd before the most beautiful girl in the world," and understood that he could die happily in her laugh that followed.

Then she said, "Hmm. So are you going to sit here or what?" and patted the seat beside her.

There was nothing astonishing to him about the way the two of them behaved after that night; it seemed a normal progression.

He never let these good times interfere with another of his strong beliefs: lives were best left mostly unexamined.

It was especially by this philosophy he was able to remove himself from any jealous effects of Ron's occasional visits to Annette, and from the obvious disdain he had for William.

Steph said, "Humph. She'll sure show you the ropes in a big hurry," and told him his Nana concurred. William saw this as a sign of support.

After many months together, William would sometimes go to Annette very early in the morning, like an intruder, quiet through the back porch of her tiny house, climb into bed and wake her softly. When the days grew longer and those mornings held a gentle light, William would always stand and watch Annette before he went home; he watched her through the spirals of bright dust caught in sunlight that came from behind muslin curtains; he watched just so he could see her there, asleep and love-worn, but as if she were swimming underwater.

There was a small moment just before William was about to die, where he understood what was happening. It was not a moment for fear, but for everything to change, and for everything to be changed for the people whose lives he had shared. Very little now had anything to do with him, except the tiny shadows spreading thickly out from somewhere behind where he stood, carried on the breath, as along isobars of hate, from the third person who had come up so quietly. There was a small moment just before William was about to die, where he understood why it was happening. He'd had no rule in place for a bad actor.

There was a graceful shift in the small moment, a freckling of shadows that spun slow as the stars across Annette's dozing form and speckled the soft afternoon light, leaving her alone and swimming.

The one sound that spoke his death reached his ears long after he began to slip through the spaces that hold the world together, and that sharp, felling of wood crack itself faded long before his smile, which never quite disappeared.

MARINE AND JONOTHAN, PLUS
CARMELITA'S JOURNAL

Journal:

My name is not Carmelita della Francesca and I am not (touch wood) an alcoholic.

Journal:

Higher education. The guy who wrote the OED quit school at fourteen and I think spoke Sanskrit and Greek. I have NO point. Times were different.

Journal:

Is it possible for curses to work among people with email and cellphones and beeping treadmills? I have them all. Also the same peacock feather I've held onto since I was fourteen — sticking out from the corners of photos and paintings and collecting dust for years. Big bad luck. I could burn it. And feel stupid and regretful. All the luck items vary from culture to culture. What if you're the product of intermarriage, like just about everybody, which genes call the luck?

Journal:

This isn't working out so well. Maybe it's my aversion to navel-gazing, and those navel-gazers I know of who keep journals. Maybe let's make this "Carmelita's Travelogue and Life Story So Far". Okay.

Journal:

I will write about the man who saved my life once.
Come to think of it, my life has been saved a few times. I wonder what it's being saved for.

   This man was by some description, very homely. Almost GQ at moments, but mostly big and ugly and way too attractive. This man inspired me to break a promise to myself only because he saved my life. It would have been easier if I'd been tied to train tracks and he'd come along and I could have just said thanks. But my near-death was more of the Nightmare Ravens tearing out your heart and soul kind. At a time when I believed I was flawed and stupid and without talent.

   I think I had a collapse or something after my first show at Jerome's gallery. Kept my real job but quit painting, quit looking at paintings, almost quit breathing. And around that same time my doctor found some nasty cell growth on my ankle of all places.

   Skin cancer. Never sunbathed, wasn't prone to moles. But they said I had it.

   I got zapped and did chemicals and meditation tapes and they said it was gone. But I walked around from then on wondering if there was a hex out there with my name on it, gamma rays with evil intentions aimed for those who were marked.

Eventually I got painting and within the year I'd set up another exhibition. Jerome was excited about the direction I'd gone, but I was terrified. There was a small, polite crowd at the opening and I had this sick smile on my face the whole time and sounded like a horse's ass in every conversation and by the end of it I was majorly bottoming out. Jerome and I decided to start some serious drinking, and he went to lock the gallery door when this couple walked in. A big ugly guy and his tiny classy wife, talking over each other and grabbing plastic glass after glass of white wine like the world was about to end and exclaiming and sticking their faces right up to my small unframed canvases and the wife finally tugging the guy's sleeve and raising her eyebrows to Jerome and me, who'd sat confused throughout all of this, saying "Zak we must go it's late, Zak we must go it's late." And the guy stomped over, grabbed my shoulders and kissed me on either cheek and then once more, pressed his fingers into me before the release and said, "It's beautiful. We will talk."

I refuse to bore myself with much more of this. I had felt doomed to being stupid and disfigured. With Zak I became brilliant and cherished and mysterious.

This is how it ended. Zak and I were to meet for an early dinner, and from there to a few hours at his friend's apartment, but it turned out that I had to work late and called him in the afternoon to cancel.

Who knows why, on the way home that evening I drove down the alley of that place where Zak and I sometimes did our loving and I stopped. A woman closed the back door of the building, got into her car and drove off. Not a big thing, but she'd forgotten to turn on her headlights and I almost went after her to remind her. But I was more interested in the light that just came on in Zak's friend's apartment. I could see Zak. The big dope hadn't bothered to close the blinds and his erection was bouncing as he hopped around trying to pull trousers on.

Where I come from, the definition of a really sleazy guy is one who cheats on his mistress.

What I really want to talk about here is not this at all. What I really want to talk about has more to do with art.

Journal:

I changed my mind. My name is Carmelita della Francesca and this is what happened.

This bit started with a round boy and a fish-faced girl.

For ages some of the guys at our high school called them the Pogos. Who knows why. I don't think pogo sticks were still around when we were teenagers. But I guess if they had been, those two would definitely have gone *spoing, spoing,* day after day, like a couple of cartoons. I mean they actually played together on that patch of lawn between the wire fences of the neighbours when they must have been at least sixteen, with half the student body making cracks at them as they walked by their house. But those two seemed so detached from us all, and there was such sadness or earnestness in the way they would watch one another and throw their ball back and forth, back and forth.

So the most I said, on the way home from school, would be *hi.*

Usually they didn't hear or pretended not to. But occasionally, maybe three times, whoever had just caught the ball would stop and tighten its mouth, but it was only the girl who, just once, said *hi* back.

There was something almost lion taming-ish about that moment.

I guess some of us were mean, but it didn't wreck them or anything. Sister Pogo was a math genius and brother Pogo got a degree and became a missionary and had a million kids before he left Canada: front page photo of them when they all left for some country. Can't remember. His sister grew up and had it in for me.

My advice to people, unless you happen to be a psychopath, is do not be too nice. You will be misconstrued or just screwed.

It would be fun to envision the present Ms. Pogo, after her peculiar beginnings, as svelte and well-married. This has been know to happen. She *is* a bit svelter and taller. But one magic transformation did take place. She became sociable in the extreme. Who knows how. She should have been skulking light-starved and toadish, illumined by her own brilliance in fusty academic rooms, whenever she wasn't yakking at podiums about integers and space-time continuums or whatever high math people like to throw back and forth to each other. On tiny front lawns.

There is a part of me that's pleased at having gone to school with Marine, who got her PhD in some physics thing and is already a Prof, but goes to concerts, plays, poetry slams, gallery openings and writes about them in a scarring, smart way.

Marine. Could be the oceans could be the soldiers.

I look at her now that we are adults, and sometimes still see her as a squeezed-lipped blowfish. Her roundness and thin mouth, startlingly bright clothes over her sallow body. She has an unusual hue, either fairness or unhealthy pallor. Maybe that's another reason she makes me think of a fish; there is a sense of water rippling around her so she changes, depending how the light is refracted. Sometimes she is a Bruegel peasant, an old-fashioned painting of an ugly child dressed like an adult. Her teeth are stunted, as if they've been worn down by a bad diet and her eyes are small, held in tight oval lids. But sometimes she can seem almost beautiful, her pale, round face with its high forehead, more like one of those Elizabethan beauties.

I recently found a word: piscivorous — fish-eating. I'm a non-piscivore. I have an aversion to eating fish, doesn't matter, tuna, trout, squid, scallops. Maybe because I almost drowned when I was four. It wasn't dying that had terrified me, I likely didn't have a real sense of death, but it was the huge disgust at being dragged to the bottom of that smelly lake with all the slime and weeds, and leeches and sharp-toothed pike that would have feasted on me. Lake was ocean. Huge and deep and populated with skulking shadowed things that bite.

Who the *hell* would name their fat grey daughter, Marine?

Marine and Jonothan

"I am tired of explaining to everyone how to spell Jonothan."

"People are stupid. Anyway, it's possible our mother is dyslectic, we'll never know."

"No."

The ball is tricoloured like the French flag and they throw and catch and throw and catch. Told to go out and play, and since they love her, they do.

"Mom has become."

They think about it.

"Very poetic."

"Po ek it."

"Po like the river or the constellation. Po plus eclectic. She does a few things at the same time."

"She thinks a lot. Gets large. Cooks red beets and stews raw meats. Po et *ick*. Like *fish* disease, Marine."

"Ick on your pencil-dick jono."

His entire being turns the colour of dinner.

School has been out for over half an hour, but they live eleven minutes away approximately from the 3:30 bell.

For the most part, the noise directed at them is noise that would happen with or without them.

A girl stops. *Why?*

Go away. She has fishnet stockings and an India cotton mini dress and short hair like a little boy. Go away. She has glasses maybe from the antique store and they're fitted with long-range lenses, they make her eyes huge. She looks scared. Why? Or is it possible she can't help it?

The girl says, "hi".

Jonothan wants them to *just* throw the ball but it's in Marine's hand, and in spite of the World at Large, she knows she has to say something or *this girl will self-destruct, never know anything, remain stupid.*

Marine says, "hi". Or thinks she has, she doesn't always know, and throws the ball to Jonothan, who never stops to say anything to any of them, the others. Not yet.

After a while they can smell cabbage and beef, slightly burnt, and they stop and go in.

There is their mother. If their mother were to sit next to the girl who stopped on the sidewalk in front of the house just then, that entire girl would be a bit narrower than their mother's thigh. Mrs. McLean has become massive. She finds it impossible to do those routine jobs that, even two years ago, were manageable. Getting on the bus downtown, doing the shopping. Last visit to the library she had to use the entrance for the handicapped. Now she can barely fit through the front door of the house. She once was a teapot, now she is a behemoth. The springs have all given up in the living room furniture. When Marine and Jonothan sit down their bums meet with either complete sag or, where plywood has been set under a cushion, complete resistance. Even some of the plywood has been shattered by Mrs. McLean, so she restricts her sitting to the sofa. Her favourite side of the sofa is crushed beyond the point where it can reassert its former shape.

Her hands are gentle and fluttery as she puts the meal on the kitchen table, tiny-boned under cupcakes of flesh. She used to cut her children's hair herself, and make wonderful desserts and sew much of their clothing, by means of accomplished designs copied from catalogues, with serged seams. There were not many people who could do what she did, and her children are well aware of her uniqueness. Also that her talents aren't necessarily ones which would be admired by the swine at school.

Her hair is thick and dark and naturally waved. Marine must wash it for her mother and helps towel her after a bi-weekly bath. Her voice, always bordering on tremolo soprano, is thinning as the flesh thickens, as if fine silver wires one by one are wearing and snapping. Even the words don't always make it to the end of her spoken thought and her children are becoming used to the singing, unattached phrases which float up to them as they do homework in their rooms.

a day just like this bluster/
the egg whites/
it was a terrible thing/
the sand they stay quite, quite

They ignore these, along with the perpetual drone of television and spurts of canned laughter, but if she's fallen asleep and the station is off the air, the high hum brings one of them down to turn it off and cover her, snoring and mountainous, with the blanket kept folded on the back of the sofa.

She is like an enormous, fruit-bearing tropical wonder which has been taken from its natural environment and fed fertilizers and hormonal supplements, until parts of her develop unchecked and begin to smother out the more delicate.

She is unable to sit at the table and sew at the machine, now out of reach for her hands and eyes at the same time. Marine's sewing skills are minimal, but she patiently constructs light cotton floor-length tents for her mother, with great rectangular sleeves. The last stretchy pants she'd sewn, large enough, she'd thought, to reupholster the entire living room suite, will not go past Mrs. McLean's knees which themselves have since disappeared under awnings of flesh.

Once a week Marine and Jonothan take a canvas bag of books to the downtown library and replace them with more for their mother. Thrillers, mysteries, romances. They buy the groceries, do the banking and try to keep up the back-yard garden (which has gradually been reduced in area by half and now grows a few root vegetables and petunias). Mrs. McLean signs the utility cheques in a careful, round, slightly ornamental hand.

Her powers of conversation have been gradually consumed by the demanding expansion of her physical self, and her children have begun to suspect she isn't reading a book the whole way through. She might say, *run out and play now.* And then get to work on the only meal of the day she prepares for them all. Sometimes she will fix the same menu three or four days in a row, and for dessert, which once might have been a German torte, baked Alaska or real angel food with boiled icing, there is now a marshmallow cookie with a waxy chocolate coat, each one presented on its own plate.

The pencil markings on the kitchen wall, to keep track of their growth, have not been added to in six years. The walls are filthy but no one has bothered.

Journal:

Carmelita is a little girl of African descent who lives in Havana, Cuba. Unofficially, she begs for a living; officially she hands out large white flowers — peonies? camellias? hydrangeas? — to the lady visitors in hopes of adoption? cash? brownie points in heaven? visions? Although she doesn't know it, one of her greater grandfathers was an Italian priest and exceptional painter of scenes recalling holy circumstances. She grew up and married, then was widowed by, a Canadian diplomat. He had suffered headaches, followed by madness, leading to total shut-down. I am not even remotely related to her.

In most ways, the Pogos were nothing to me during that stretched out multilayered desperate time of life, where nobody is supposed to exist unless they dress and talk like you do. My friends and I were reading some book that recommended things to enjoy while smoking pot, but my mother confiscated it and I had hell to pay with the guy who'd bought it in the first place. I gave him my *Siddhartha* but he still was never the same to me. And I felt awful because my parents gave me that one for my birthday. And the guy who ended up with my first Hermann Hesse, I don't even remember his name and wouldn't know him now from Adam. But I was once in agonized love with him for way too long. I would take any little thing he'd say to me, bring it home to dissect and cherish and have what I thought at the time were wild sexual fantasies about him. Freud was right, young woman are the *horniest*. Or I think that was Freud. That right there is my problem. I have a slippery or oil-slicked kind of mind, where sometimes even the commonest of nouns roll around like ball bearings and I have to run after them and pick up several before I find the right one. Some people have Velcro minds. I would assume that Marine is one of those. I can read her reviews and have no trouble going: yeah! Exactly! Or Bullshit, get a grip, Marine. But if I had to repeat anything beyond the most fundamental sense of what she'd written, I'd be screwed. Or even have to explain what I thought about the same book or movie. Unless I'd been drinking and was with friends, I'd sound like a ten year old.

They were a weird pair. And I didn't have to walk past that house, but I made a point of it. Only reason I discovered them first time was because I had to avoid someone else.

But in my mistaken young brain, I had thought they'd be on that lawn forever for me to go past at my convenience deciding whether to stop and see if one of them noticed me. First time they weren't there was not a big deal. But a week later I was consumed with collective guilt — we'd driven them indoors, they are ashamed and confused by us, the world. Then I saw them a while later, coming out of a Fellini movie at 2 a.m. Even then I couldn't imagine they'd actually wanted to be at that theatre, and I created reasons for them — they must have a brutal, drunken father and had to stay out of the house and out of his way until he collapsed, alone and raging. I mean, nobody went out with their brother or sister. And what were kids like that doing at a Fellini?

I graduated a year ahead of Marine. Many of my friends were already well into university Art or Drahma degrees and I expected to be joining them. Then I took a long look at the student loan thing and studio classes demanding gallons of various paints and ten kinds of paper and a roll of canvas, and having to read two novels a day plus attend rehearsals after hours. And I shamed myself by taking a job as a temporary secretary. Only in those days would this be allowed. I could type less than 40 wpm, but they liked my phone voice. I should have been a sex counsellor or psychic advisor but I never knew those jobs were there and would I really have had enough drahma to pull it off? Regrets, I've had more than a few Mr. Sinatra.

Marine chopped 2 letters from her name. This is her byline: Mari. No last name. What is gone, I wonder. *Ne* negate? Necromancy? Negligent? Neh? *Ne* is the sound of grunting or struggle or bad dreams. And the chopping of her name is now common knowledge. The paper did a thing on her, and she said her mother was French, like that explains *shit*. And that her father must have had the final say in their names, but he died when she was young and her mother, a well-read and very spiritual person was the true influence.

Spoing, spoing.

I get urges to make contact with unusual animals, for example, orb spiders. They've got webs that would hold a small kitten and strands of so-called silk that they connect overnight as walkways to a back door, steel cable quality, so when I open the door it forms a half loop and the spider runs to the nuclear-attack-ready web, and I don't know whether it's to escape the big disturbance or to wait and eat it. And I admire the strength and size of her, her usefulness in sucking up moths and caragana bugs; the white button mushroom which is her bulk; the complete nerve in setting up by a constantly used door. But I really just want us to have a reassuring talk.

So. I was a temp, though my first job lasted over a year. And my phone voice worked okay, and all kinds of difficult calls were switched over to me. Deceiving voices work both ways, though. There was a lovely, entertaining middle-aged woman who phoned regularly from a top client's office and it was months before she said: Now I know who you are, you're that cute little girl with the headscarf and black stockings, I'll see you tomorrow when I bring Christmas chocolates for the girls. And *he* winked at me the next day, a really gay dark-haired designer guy heaped with gold foil boxes. Oops. And *darn* when I got a good look at him.

Does my love life have to be a part of this, Carmelita? She isn't sure.

I keep wanting to write only these words: *Spoing Spoing*. Like the guy doing Redrum Redrum or whatever on his typewriter. Shine? no, he was the crazy pianist. Middle aged what's his name, Robert De Niro, Al Pacino. Nuttier. Christopher Walken Alan Arkin Donald Sutherland. Shacked up with three witches. Jack Nicholson.

Spoing spoing. Murder by pogo stick. Middle of the desert, sidewinders and Gila monsters and shape-shifting Navajos skirting the edge of the picture while victim is held by (thongs, rocks, books, ex-husbands, slain artists), gradually worn and whittled and squished inch by inch.

Trouble is I can't tell if I'm killer or victim.

I've got a terrible evil urge to make it all up from here. But we all know biography, esp. autobiography, is fiction anyhow. So you'll never, never know. (Insert maniacal laughter)

Once, I tried to kill me. When living in an unintentionally German Expressionist apartment. Between men. Well, the between of course assumes there was one waiting impatiently for me. The real between was between the former and recent latter. I'd shut the doors leading from the kitchen — one to the entrance porch, the other to the barely living room and barely bedding room. I rolled up towels and dish cloths and blocked the openings. The window was always so hard to open I just closed it, knowing it was hermetically sealed.

There was an off-white 40s or 50s gas stove that had to be fired up with a wooden match, minor explosion style. First I put on Verdi's *Requiem*, taped off CBC, but couldn't stand to die by that. Tried an old Pentangle record but it just made me want to drink rosehip tea with honey, same for Buffalo

Springfield. All the newer old stuff, some one-album-to-their-names folk or funk bands, got on my nerves so bad I decided it was a sign for dignified death amidst utter silence. My apartment was at the back of the building and most noise coming from outside was drowned by clanging hot water pipes. There I was — showered, mascara-ed, clean underwear and my favourite unbleached muslin sylph dress — in a small tight room with the gas jets going, oven door wide open. I was at peace. And this is what went through my mind, my last thoughts, as I *knelt by the stove and laid my head on the open door: Like Edith Piaf. No. She was a singer. Like the poet, Edith Piaf. Not Piaf. Edith . . . Plaff. Edith Plaff. No, Plath!* Yeah, that's it, like Edith Plath. My brain had thuddenly acquired a lithp. And I started to laugh. Laughing gas like rotten eggs and maybe yeah my eyes were going weird on me. Yeth by George, they were. And thtill I could not remember that poet's name.

So, pretty much between laughing and being really annoyed with my disability with words, I opened the doors and then fiddled with the dial thing on the stove and turned off the gas. Even as I laughed and staggered I wondered whether I needed to call someone, like an ambulance or the doctor's to make an appointment for a test to discover how many brain cells might have been fried.

I didn't do either. I did eventually phone a kind of manic friend of mine who was studying jazz piano and let her talk for two hours about aquasize, judo, the skinny native guy who ran across the street and kicked her foot while she was burned out after class waiting for a bus, the one black spider she thought she'd killed while we were talking because she booted a box of papers out of the way not wanting it to crawl in there, and the various stages of its curled-upness and recoveredness until she finally lost track of it and said shit I got to go maybe it's under my pant leg or something. And she hung up, never hearing my strange tale. She'd been the right person to call.

Carmelita would have just ordered in some Chinese and written a play.

I wish I could say that the world became clear and bright after the suicide, and that I had revelations and epiphanies. But in spite of coming out laughing, there was a large, blurred period spanning months and months where anything I can now recall, I'd rather not.

Marine and Jonothan

Marine is sixteen and Jonothan fifteen when Mrs. McLean tells them, in her sweet, rippling voice, to go out and play. They look at each other.

Marine says, "We thought we'd go to a movie so don't make dinner for us, all right?"

Their mother is already at the edge of the sofa, readying herself for the great hoist which will bring her to her feet and into her slippers. She looks at Marine in a very clear and, Marine hopes she reads it right, happy way. She says, "What a lovely idea, I'll just fix myself a can of soup."

At which point begins the emancipation of the younger McLeans.

There are many places for Marine and Jonothan to go, but most are unsuited for them or they are unsuited for the place. They know, rightly, they are not yet fish or fowl. To look at them it is hard to know if they are children or youth, as they appear pubescent in both fashion and development. They will not consider hanging out at the park for instance, where cigarettes and drugs are passed around and frisbees thrown and young people bunch and talk and listen to bands on weekends.

They explore. Movies on Saturday afternoons are half price. And they watch everything they can. There are two alternative movie houses which for a dollar ninety-nine show foreign and second run films at midnight. If Mrs. McLean is aware they are out so late she doesn't comment. Gradually they become familiar with particular directors and may see the same movie several times, sometimes just to settle arguments but more often because they are determined to understand it.

Marine and Jonothan come home late from school one day and their mother is watching *Jeopardy* and laughing softly.

"Were you here at lunch?" demands Marine, of Jonothan.

"Were you?"

They go, together, to the sofa. There is a dark stain on the yellow nylon fabric and almost to the waist of their mother's light blue granny print dress. They are afraid she is in some state of delirium.

But she sees them and says, "Something is wrong and I need a bath."

Marine takes her upstairs and understands that everything is now beyond the three of them. She will ask the school nurse for phone numbers. And lie quite a lot.

Their mother continues to bloom until she is grown beyond the confines of the sofa and the narrow stairwell to her bedroom.

They don't drink and they don't smoke. They have dressed in Sally Ann years before it becomes the thing to do, and more and more run into some hip kid from school as they all rummage through the same racks of wrinkly discards. They discover that aside from the Public Art Gallery, there are others. Free of charge. Marine is especially drawn to installations, and will go back and forth between the artists' statements and the piles of gravel, photographs, dismembered toys, men's suits, things that float in formaldehyde, and so on. She also loves the most impenetrable of canvases, layered and heavy and dark. Jonothan is more a landscape, figurative man. And makes no apologies for it. "Non-representational art," he asserts, "tells us nothing about the human condition."

"Oh, so it follows that you only like music with words," Marine says, nastily.

She is older, now in her last semester of high school, and can still make him squirm and blush.

He is screaming inside almost every day at the thought of being alone next year in that wretched, soul-sucking building surrounded by hundreds of nitwits and jocks and centrefold girls and guys that fight and hardly anyone to talk to beyond: What's on the exam? Can I borrow your eraser?

But he replies to Marine, "That is the stupidest thing I've ever heard and you know it is."

He is stranded after all, next fall, when Marine takes her full scholarship to the university.

Behind his desk, in Latin class, sits a very quiet girl. She has been so quiet the past few years Jonothan barely knew she was there, and has to think hard to summon her name: Cindy.

There is a tap on his shoulder, and a voice: "Can I please borrow your eraser?"

He turns around with his practised scowl.

The girl recoils just a little at his attitude, narrows her eyes and chews her bottom lip.

It takes Jonothan a minute to digest it all. Before this moment, if he has ever exerted an influence over any human besides his mother and sister, it has gone unnoticed. He has been a brute. How is that possible? To make amends he becomes a brave man and scowls at her again, really hard, and says, "Say please and Simon says."

She gets it and grins. "Please and Simon says."

His face and scalp burn so hard he takes a long time pretending to find the eraser, and when he turns to give it to her she is still smiling and now bright pink. A while later she taps him and gives it back, and borrows it twice more before the bell rings.

There are at least two other recreational venues for Jonothan to explore at his age. The New Christian Youth keep themselves very busy, and Cindy has brought Jonothan to them.

Mrs. McLean, in the meantime, is now confined to the main floor where a bed has replaced the sofa, and she has a commode and a visiting nurse. Her hair is still dark and thick, but cut much shorter for convenience, and her melodic phrases are reduced to one or two words. She sings

lovely/
P.D. James/

to the/

spoons

One time only, in the entire year and a half the nurse's aide has been to visit, Mrs. McLean sits up in surprise and speaks. She says: "Do you know, there were certain occasions when father was pressed for time, he just wrung the hen's neck and popped it off like a cork. Can you imagine! Like a cork from a bottle."

The nurse's aide sits down on the nearest easy chair, hard, due to plywood. "Is that a fact. Well, we always had the block and two nails, you know, with an axe until they came out with the tin cones. You know. Upside-down."

But Mrs. McLean is snoring.

She continues to expand, spilling outwards soft and pale until her fingernails are the only intact remainder. Her face looks out at them, wise and difficult to focus on, like the man in the moon's, a hint of a face, the cartilage of nose buried with just two nostrils open to let in the air. Her eyes are black pearls gleaming from within pillowing lids. An infant's mouth.

There is no explanation as to what feeds her; like an air fern, she seems to thrive without nourishment.

Marine is in her fourth year at university and Jonothan his third, when one afternoon they are both, separately, drawn away from class. They meet, as if by chance, at the bus stop.

"Our mother has become very interesting," Marine says slowly.

Only for a split of a second, though Jonothan believes he is now made from new and better cloth, does he try to thwart the rest of this conversation.

"She is become poetic," he says.

They go home together, knowing exactly how things will be.

There is some debate from Jonothan, who has a concern with cremation being essentially a heathen practice. But Marine has already, discreetly, visited the funeral home and its downstairs display of coffins — polished oak or spruce, done up with shirred satin, and the cost of which was beyond what the three of them lived on for months — finding nothing which could possibly contain their mother. She asked about having something special built, and was at first met with puzzlement. Would she like something fancier, or more impermeable to the ravages of time, metal or stone perhaps?

Bigger, she said.

They would have to construct a small hut and then find a horde of barbarians to carry it. It must be ashes to ashes.

Jonothan gives in, although he has a metaphorical twinge concerning hell-fire. And credit to the Youth and their families, a respectably large and joyous crowd observes their mother's service.

Walking back down the aisle of the funeral home, first in line to the waiting limo and there to the committal of Mrs. McLean's ashes, Marine sees an unexpected face at the edge of a pew near the back. A young woman with spiked hair and glasses, wearing gothic dramatic black, and looking straight at her. What the hell, Marine wonders, would possess *her* to be here? But she can't quite place who *her* is.

Journal:

Carmelita, you self-contained darling. You who are perfect of vision and eyesight, you who are perfect of form. You winnower of everything to do with my life.

It was several years ago when I found myself at the same event as Marine. I'd seen her around a few times, but this was much different. This happened to be a roast, by invitation only, in honour of a local poet I'd come to know quite well, and damned if Marine wasn't one of the guest speakers. She still seemed to have that quality of being one degree separated from the rest of the world, as if what anybody said or thought about her wouldn't even register. I was nervous for her anyway, worried that people would think she was extremely weird. But it turned out I was about the only one in the audience who didn't know *this* Marine. There were a couple of whoops and even scattered clapping as she made her way to the front. And she was witty and unassuming and somehow looked so *right* up there with the microphone, stringy hair and wacky clothes and all. Afterwards I tried a couple of times to talk with her, or at least say hi. But somebody always got in the way.

A couple of weekends later I was doing my usual job search, and in the local paper I read an obit, more like a two-line notice for a Memorial Service, and the deceased in question was Mrs. Mary McLean, mourned by *daughter, Dr. Mari McLean and son Jonothan McLean.* I went, okay, they had a mother.

So there I was at a very small Funeral Home chapel for the service. It was a young crowd mostly, and I wondered where all the middle-aged couples that most parents gather around them were, the co-workers and neighbours and relatives. It was hard at first to find Marine and her brother, but I saw them in the front pew as they stood to make room for someone. Marine was in a really awful tweedy suit and her hair was tied back crookedly with a thick blue elastic.

They'd barely sat down when the first preacher introduced a second preacher and everything turned strange. The second guy had a face like a basset hound, and a ratty moustache, and he was kind of slow-dancing with his voice rising and falling and praising and sorrowing. I had already prepared myself in my own way before I'd left home, shared a prayer and then a pleasant word with The Lady, and didn't know if I should be shocked at this dramatic stuff. I kept my eye on the back of Marine's head, which she'd held perfectly still, and she didn't react to any of the pulpit prompts. A certain percentage of the guests or mourners stood once in a while and raised their arms. They said yes, yes, and a-a-*amen*. Like sex.

It was finally all done; dreary canned music started to play and Marine was up the first possible chance and leading the parade down centre aisle. She had a determined look, like she refused to let anything get to her or think about what lay ahead. Anyhow. She was marching toward me and that water-ripple thing happened. She turned into a beauty, an unusual woman caught out of her real time and place. I could almost see her wearing pearls and brocade and possibly facing a sentence to a nunnery.

Lady, I whispered, protect her. Something like that. Maybe it was bless her.

And Marine looked up and saw me. She looked right into my eyes and her brows tucked toward her nose a little, and then she turned away and kept going.

I knew that somehow she'd heard me.

Tectonic plates. There they are, deep under the rocks and dirt and roots and cities. Just waiting, inch shift by inch shift, to do some real damage.

Doesn't matter. You can attend your aerobics classes and pluck your brows and eat lots of vegetables and visit the whatever circles of knowledge. There are forces at play so simple, natural, and accidental that nobody can figure them out and see them coming. You can tell yourself what a good, caring person you are. You can tell yourself you're a success. But if any joker makes it through life on his own terms, it's just pure dumb luck.

Marine and Jonothan

When Marine reaches the chapel doors she steps back slightly, forcing Jonothan to move ahead of her. She is vaguely, and irritatingly, aware of Cindy at their heels and knows that Cindy will probably not have the nerve to follow her into the waiting limousine, but might easily attach herself to Jonothan. It is essential that they be allowed to form themselves together into brother and sister, as they are.

Marine ushers Jonothan into the back seat, then places herself right beside the door and motions to the funeral director that she is ready to receive the unadorned box which is now their mother, complete and condensed. The director has control on the remains and continues to keep control while he places them carefully onto her lap, even as her own hands have clasped the box the whole way down. She is somehow touched by his care in doing this with her, knowing he is being cautious in the event of an emotional daughter who might let the ashes slip. Then she nods and the car door shuts them in, and Cindy out.

Marine wonders what should be said; this is the first circumstance ever where she is lost for words with her brother.

There are the subtle smells of the limousine's mauve-grey velour interior, and of Jonothan, who in the past year has developed what she identifies as a man's odour, including muscular tension, scraped beard, and something close to salt.

Her mother rests — now strangely heavy — on her lap, contained in the plainest of boxes. Marine and Jonothan want it to be like this. Plain box for plain home containing the indefinable Mrs. McLean, whose ashes they will soon mix with the turned earth, as they requested, in her allotted space at the cemetery.

At first Marine thinks they are already moving. There is a spreading and fraying of time. The long line of people outside seems to stand still and become smaller as the car draws away, but in fact it is the people who are filing towards their cars

Then they *are* moving. They are being driven, locked in the back of a thundering limousine, at horrific speed. Marine has heard of situations such as this. Entire families killed on the way to a loved one's funeral. She is probably going to die. The traffic circle leading out of town is dense and blaring and they fly along it. Marine wants to look out the rear window but resists, afraid of what she might see. How can the motorcade possibly keep up with them?

They have reached the overpass. It is transformed into a long, sharply ascending sky-bridge, impossibly narrow, with only a low ridge of cement on either side. She stares out her window, far down onto silent, lazy clouds which drift over canyons. The vertigo almost causes her to scream out loud.

If the car were to stop a person would have to go across that awful space alone and would have to get on hands and knees and crawl down the centre because if they stand and walk their steps might take a lopsided line and they will be gone.

The driver slows.

Marine realizes she has been gripping the box hard enough that one corner is creased. She forces her hands to relax, but the box has become so light it begins to float away and she presses firmly on the top until it finally comes to rest, solid on her lap.

The late autumn sun strobes harsh through a barricade of trees which edge the winding lanes of the cemetery. She blinks away and breathes deep.

Words now reach her.

Jonothan is speaking quietly. Marine knows that if Jonothan hears nothing from her, he will continue playing with an idea for a while by himself, so she lets him talk on before she focuses and listens, waiting for the right moment to respond.

And she keeps listening and wonders at first if she must still be caught in that waking dream, until with a sickening pain, she understands that his words are not directed to her. The phrases she hears are *figurative*, as in Jonothan's interpretation of the term: both pictorial and with a confident metaphysical aspect, and are definitely addressed to God.

Marine is alone.

They are at the scene of committal.

She had only thought she understood something before this moment, but now she truly knows the rightness of it: there are many options to reality. As in, reality is optional.

She is here with Jonothan and with others known and mostly unknown, and most importantly with their physical mother in a much smaller state than could ever have been imagined before. Every single soul at the event will experience reality in a very different way and Marine herself experiences it in many. She is curious, for example, if any remains were forgotten, and whether a crumb of bone dust left behind could find its way to this site — swept into a cuff, then fallen to a gutter, then blown onto a jacket, then brushed off in a florist's shop, then packaged with a funeral arrangement which would eventually be delivered to this area and the crumb would hop on another current of air to mix with the rest.

She is certain that if such things are important to her mother, they will come about.

She is aware of how little she knows this person who was her brother. It's as if they happened to share the same childhood vision once, even at times shared the same mind. She is suddenly in awe of the determination he must possess to have been able to cut her away from him as he has. She wonders if his burning dedication to God and Cindy could possibly hold the intensity of discovery she experiences at school. It is hard to imagine the attraction otherwise.

The quiet Cindy is again at Jonothan's side. She is beatific, the only word Marine can find for her, although she wishes to despise her. Cindy should be dowdy, frumpy, too small in the nose, too flat of heels, too ignorant of foreign films. But Cindy not only is glowing of face, she keeps her weepy eyes to herself and doesn't impose them on Marine, and confines her adoration of Jonothan to one squeeze of his arm.

Marine would like to discuss all of this with Mrs. McLean, but she cannot honestly recall the last conversation she had with her mother. Or the last time she thought there was any need for one.

Marine feels blessed at this realization: she has been reared very well within unusual circumstances.

When the time comes for her and Jonothan to mix the ashes with the earth, the small crowd draws back. Marine now sees the inherent awkwardness of the compromise they came to in dealing with the remains: Jonothan in a suit, herself in skirt and nylons, having to open the box without it seeming like a birthday party. They kneel at the graveside and Marine grimly dumps out the ashes, and they dig in, lifting the dirt and folding it all together until the surface is dark. She has no idea how long it has taken but the whole thing felt more like gardening than worship.

They rise.

No matter how many times Marine brushes her knees, the stain will not leave. Jonothan has two muddy crusts on his dress pants, but doesn't bother to touch them.

On the return drive to the tea, Cindy is sharing their back seat.

Journal:

This song is stuck in my head right now, and as usual I can't repeat more than a couple of lines and I'll remember what band it is tomorrow, when I should be doing something important

Mama told me not to come Ah ah ah
Mama told me not to come Ah ah She said
That ain't no way to have fun Oh oh oh
That ain't no way to have fun

My mom was in such a hurry I popped out two months early and should have died. Maybe she was trying to save me from life, in advance.

There is something that really, really pisses me off. I hate writing about anything that pisses me off so bad.

This is the thing. I know Marine grew up kind of poor and funny-looking and should be applauded for her accomplishments. But *her* real job lasts eight months a year. She makes more bucks in that time than I make at a real job in three years. And she gets a hell of a holiday where she can trip around and do her art critic thing. I work after work, I work until four in the morning sometimes, I took evening classes and begged student discounts from art suppliers and was routinely turned down for grants and went through a marriage before I found a gallery that would take me on.

Marine saw my first show. She wasn't even at the opening. But she saw my show. Her review of it spent a lot of energy knocking the concept of personal mythology in art, and she used words like hodge-podge, floundering and vapid, and then threw in some backhanded encouragement.

Basically she called my work sloppy and myself ignorant.

Why would Marine say those things? She who raved over a show which consisted of a huge room, empty but for an ironing board in one corner and diagonally from it, a single shelf lined with jars of jelly beans. And another she loved, a group of five canvases that were pretty much variations on shellacked vomit.

Marine

Now that her mother and Jonothan are both gone, Marine has discovered that no matter how much she does she can always accommodate something more. Her mother had almost completely filled her heart and her brother had almost completely filled her soul.

The void they left seems infinite.

Six years have passed since the last moment she and Jonothan were truly brother and sister. That was the afternoon they entered their house and found their mother alone, eyes closed, and finally emptied of life. For a long time they stood and watched her, not quite accepting this complete silence from even such a subtle woman. It had seemed that a long reed, finer than light, had been siphoning her essence away from them so gradually that she might have continued to lie there and grow as she had, for another century. Defying all laws in protest of what was being stolen from her.

Twelve years have passed since Marine received her first scholarship. She is conscious of having made some superficial changes since then, mainly those which were useful in presenting herself. When she was first on tenure track — on the advice of the only faculty member she actually talked with — she made several trips to a store which outfitted professional women. It was a grim experience, but the result was an alternate wardrobe of what she called University Clothes.

It is a rare moment when Marine will bother to study herself, in the mirror, or otherwise. She is looking now in the mirror, very carefully. She concentrates on her hair, which has grown past the middle of her back but is ragged. When was it last cut? Her skin is fine-grained and dullish, but never prone to break-out. She decides she will not try makeup now; it has never been an option.

She is examining herself because she needs an explanation for something which has happened. There is a man.

Although she understands that the comparison she is about to make is possibly incestuous, she can't help it. The man is absolutely nothing like Jonothan. He is an Armenian, unusually tall and wide and unabashedly sexual, with a huge sloping-to-a-ski-jump nose, and a wicked, offensive laugh which he directs almost randomly to individuals who end up either crushed or elated.

The only thing he has in common with her brother is, they both are married and have uncountable children.

She chides herself at "uncountable". It has just been too painful or impossible to sustain enthusiasm. Her lack of interest began when Jonothan and Cindy presented their second, a son. As if some biological joke had been played, little Elijah followed his sister Mary by eleven months, the same span between Marine and Jonothan. Three more children have followed and their parents take great pleasure in deciding on names for the ones in the wings, waiting to be born to them.

Journal:

Carmelita has decided to bring her extensive knowledge of flowers and human nature to a freer country populated with all kinds of real men, many of them imported. Canada is a marvelous place for a beautiful widow of seriously artistic ancestry and a government pension. Carmelita would have turned up her nose at the man who once saved my life.

Marine

When the forty-two-year-old Armenian first tells Marine how beautiful she is, she thinks he is, without a doubt, a madman.

After many months, she decides they are equal parts of a *strange attractor*, caught in a complex pattern of behaviour within a definitely chaotic system. Her times with him are separate and very different from anything she has known, and when they meet it's as if she enters a black and white film of unknown director. She experiences a sensation not unfamiliar to many people: Marine becomes an actor in her own life.

The Armenian is always sweet and satisfied after their lovemaking, but other times he says things such as "I think you are only making a study of me," or "I am your specimen." Marine doesn't reply to these; she hasn't been offered any lines that feel right.

One evening, in his passion, he calls her by a name which is neither hers nor his wife's. The name is not a part of any equation she will accept.

She considers becoming hotly embarrassed for having messed together poetry with mathematics, and ending in such a classically stupid and naive scene as this. Instead she forces the importance of their affair to wither in an instant, throws on her clothes and leaves him half-coital. His entreaties follow her down the hall and can still be heard, although muffled, as she reaches the alley door of his

MARINE AND JONOTHAN, PLUS CARMELITA'S JOURNAL

friend's borrowed apartment. She drives away, deter-
minedly planning the morning's lecture.

Journal:

I've got it cased for Midsummer's Day. It will happen at the
little zoo on the edge of the city where all sorts of birds
waltz around and look glorious. Huge, odd-coloured,
fluffy, iridescent, each of them self-importantly silly and
lucky to be where nothing more dangerous than popcorn
happens. I will take my peacock feather and go past the
Japanese bridge where it's shady and mossy and the
raptors' cries are distant and the puddle-ducks zip around
their pond, and I'll wait until nobody is on that path and
I'll drop the feather there, to become just one more
among the rest. And it will be free to do whatever feathers
are meant to when they're left alone.

SPOOR

GEORGE MIGHT HAVE FOUND A BETTER PICTURE OF ROSE for the personals last week, on her birthday. *Lordy Lordy Look Who's Forty*. There was his little sister's high school picture in grainy black and white: dark-rimmed glasses and shoulder length hair, huge lapels, a goofy scarf tie. He'd phoned every radio station, too. "This song's goin' out to Rose for her *Fiftieth* birthday." That was mean, though he figured it was funny at the time, but she was so broken up about turning forty he couldn't resist. Picked the hokiest tunes he could think of. But not the Joni Mitchell, the one he'd often hummed over the years, privately. *I think of Rose my heart begins to tremble . . .*

Could have been written for his sister. Rose Who Knows. Rosita who Nosita.

He phones her at the store. She answers in her gravelly voice, "Ya we got Robin Hood in a bag, think we ought to let him out? Pretty old, Georgie, old and stale. And, oh yeah, I heard the radio this morning and so'd half the people coming in here today."

He imagines Rose sitting by the till, sucking back her fourth smoke before lunch. Small town, no anti-smoking bylaws there yet. Rose counts out kids' nickels and pennies, puts their candy in tiny brown bags, knows everybody by name, sets her smoke in the ashtray if she needs to run back and slice bacon for a customer, half the time leaves it hanging out the corner of her mouth while she punches the till. Never seems to get in her eyes. He couldn't do it, smoke always goes straight up his nose, burns out a sinus. Smoking is something Rose is real good at.

"Come for supper, Georgie."

"Anybody else going to be there, planning you a surprise party or something?"

"Not I'm aware of."

Never knew with Rose. People were always showing up; neighbours appear on her back step in tears, and if it's real bad she gets out the single malt scotch she hides under the sink.

He's glad she seems to be off her vegetarian kick for now. Vegetables are okay, even his dog eats them, but Rose would serve mountains of gut-expanding spiced-up chick peas and lentils and brown rice. You could run a windmill off one of those dinners. George figures a human needs red meat to function right. Pound of flesh. "Shit Rose, haven't you got anything else?" "There's hot dogs in the freezer." Rose somehow didn't count them as meat.

Rose moved out to that little town sixteen years ago, married a trucker named Scott. "Why get married, Rose?" George had asked. "Just stay a bit, see how it works out." But she had a feeling about him, and with Rose that was it. She moved on it. Any feeling. "Besides," she'd told George, "it's a small place, I don't want anybody treating me like dirt because I'm not married." A rare give-in to convention for Rose. George thought the guy seemed okay, maybe a bit gushy, figured he could give Rose "stability". What was the point, she never needed it before. Of course it was cats and dogs from day one with them screaming and swearing and crying. Well, Rose did the crying. She hardly ever cleaned house, and cooked when it suited her, and liked flowers better than potatoes. Tracked half the garden in on her bare feet. Drove her husband right up the wall. George was relieved when it turned out Scott had a girlfriend in Montana, where he trucked to regularly. They were all happy when he finally moved in with her instead.

But George was amazed Rose wanted to stay in that nowhere place. Maybe that's what her feeling was about, had nothing to do with marrying Scott, but knowing somehow she would like it — oiled roads and rows of cottagey houses, old guys driving tractors to the bar because the Mounties took their licences away, kids pedalling trikes and plastic toys around the streets.

This is where Rosita, who'd spent a couple summers in San Francisco during her late teens, ended up. But the world seemed to come to her in this backroad safe prairie place; the world kept on coming to Rosita. So George has to ask Rose who else might be there because he tries to avoid weirdness.

He gets to work before noon. Makes up a batch of caesar dressing, starts the beef sauce, kids around with the young dishwasher. For a few hours he helps sweat out meal after meal, sends the washer out for more ice, crosses one of the Specials off the menu.

On the way home, he has a hard time feeling his feet on the sidewalk, and the houses are on a slight tilt. Heads to the 7-11 for smokes. If this was Park Avenue he'd just have to get around the corner to collect his two hundred dollars, but he's got to work a whole week for that.

As always, tendrils of Rosita weave around what he's doing, scents of her, worries of her, tripping him up.

George never figured it was Californian drugs that got to his sister — it was Elsie, Elsie the spook queen of Brazil, as George called her behind her back.

She's messing with your head, Rosie, quit seeing that woman. But Rose was still a little girl, no different in California wearing India cotton and ankle bracelets and strands of tiny beads, than she had been hanging off of George in the city, when she had the green cowgirl hat with a whistle and her nickel-plated six gun. Figured she was a sharp-shooter little tough girl who could take aim and duck behind her big brother. Always like that. Do the damage and run to George.

He goes home to change, collapses into the armchair. His dog flops across his feet, but sits up suddenly to scratch. "Dammit Dusky, you got fleas again. Shit, there's something up my pant leg. You know fleas love me don't you, bad girl. Their tiny brains say, 'well it ain't dog but I'll just chow down for fun.' Don't look so picked on, nothing worse than a bath is coming at you. Oh yes." He rubs her ear, says very deliberately: "You like baths don't you." She starts to quiver. "Look, got one." He has the flea pinched between thumb and forefinger, rolls it up hard, then opens his hand. The flea blasts off, untouched.

"People ought to be built like that."

Last year Dusky got a woodtick behind her ear, and George gripped the thing near its head with tweezers, and then dropped it with revulsion on his old linoleum kitchen floor. It landed on its back, legs wiggling and wiggling.

George put a match to the tick, watched it crackle and hiss into a black crumb.

"I have to wonder why some creatures even are. Bloodsuckers, what's the point?" Dusky grins at him. He starts singing "There is a rose in Spanish Harlem". Rosita, some kind of Spanish name, George could never understand what was up with their mother when she'd named her. Although she was pretty hot on Dezi Arnez at the time. Cubans are Spanish or something, aren't they? He remembers their mother even looking kind of like Lucille Ball when they were little, shit, she had extra eyelashes and the whole routine. Used to draw her eyebrows on thick, don't see that on women any more. *Find my mules, Georgie,* never thought of it until now. Her blue slippers being mules.

He has great affection for his mother, but didn't appreciate being made legal guardian of Rosita when he was nineteen, although guarding her was nothing new. Their mother crushed into the steering wheel of her red 1967 Mustang convertible. The freeway lamp standard bent, not broken. A line of false eyelash jolted from a lid, fluttering on her dead-still right cheekbone. The horn blaring. Not that he knows the details for sure, but it couldn't have been any different.

She used to give him lunch money when she remembered, so he could go to the café a couple blocks from his high school, where he'd meet Rosita. Rosita hanging off him all the time. *Watch your sister now, Georgie.* Always.

Rosita hiding now under her thick framed glasses — she hardly even needed them, but it kept boys away — and frumpy shirts, beat-up shoes. George was growing his hair long then, sitting in black light coffeehouses and dropping acid. Then one day it seemed, but it couldn't have been one day, Rose wore black eyeliner instead of black frames, and her dark wavy hair looked wild and cool instead of uncared-for. He noticed her mentioning lots of things becoming too heavy for her head, and his friends talking to her instead of to him. Couldn't count on Rose going out with a girlfriend, or watching television with their mother, because Rose was with him again. Listening to the same folk singers, going to the same bars.

"Maybe I've led you down the garden path, Rosie," he had said.

"Don't be an idiot, I'm capable of finding my own path." She'd ditched him for a bit after that, but eventually called from California and asked him to come. That's when he found out about Elsie.

But he didn't stay long.

"Come home," he'd urged Rose. She'd said, "Soon."

He drives out the north end of the city, past the steel warehouses and the implement dealers and rows of trucks and heavy equipment.

He misses the turnoff to the main highway on purpose. He likes the surprises of grid roads, plus doesn't need to use the overdrive which quits on him regularly.

Of course nothing to do with the overdrive makes his truck overheat a few miles from Rose's. He lifts the hood, ducks steam, finds where the clamp broke off a hose; must have happened a while ago to run dry like it has. He grabs the smoke from behind his ear, locks up and heads off to his sister's.

Half an hour later he reaches behind his ear the fifth time for a smoke he's already finished, and remembers with annoyance the pack sitting on the seat of his truck. But that tight spot between scalp and ear has a kind of buzz on it, like something should be there. Maybe something bit him. He rubs around and feels nothing. He considers it might be a virus. Behind his ear. From smoking. Rose says you're supposed to wash your hands, if you're a smoker, before you touch tomatoes on the vine. You can give tomatoes some sort of tobacco virus.

He sees the lights from Rose's town flickering a mile or so off.

If it was the end of the world, he'd be the last guy to know it. Not a vehicle in sight. Could be abducted by aliens and not a soul to witness. That thought cheers him up. He kicks the deep dust and notices a - - - - - of bird tracks, so he follows the crazy weaving pattern around until each little print is obliterated.

Eight in the evening. Mist appears in the hollows of the fields, silking around the muffled edges of poplar bluffs.

He gets to Rose's, and she's all fired up to look after his truck before they eat, but he bums a smoke first, and has a beer and they eat up sausage sliced into scalloped potatoes.

"Didn't feel like cooking much tonight, huh Rose?"

"I thought you'd be here earlier, I was doing something quick. It's been ready two hours."

They climb into her old Datsun with a bleach bottle filled with water and a piece of wire to clamp the hose. They forget a flashlight so George does repairs by the flame of Rose's disposable lighter.

He lets the truck run a few minutes, then follows the Datsun back to Rose's for another beer, watches the temperature gauge, which is fine. The night's cooled off quite a bit.

"Almost anybody else would be nagging at me for showing up so late for their birthday, and not coming to see them more often, and keeping them up on a working night, but not you."

"I'll do your cards."

"No thanks."

"You're restless, Georgie, like there's something's going on."

"Nothing going on. Except Dusky's got fleas."

"You look worried."

"I should look worried. The truck could have died before it did, and I'd be out in the middle of acreage country, have to go past somebody's Rottweiller to knock at the door to use the phone, if someone was even home. And they might not let me in and it'd be up the road to the next place and maybe the same thing. Might have walked fifteen miles tonight instead of three, and the three damn near killed me."

"Your hair's getting long. You growing it?"

"Hadn't thought about it." But he thinks about it then, and decides he'll get it cut tomorrow. Elsie had liked his hair. Too much. She'd weave her long fingers through it, slide it between her lips. Massage his scalp. It makes him sick.

Elsie mostly wore her hair up, thick and teased in a classy kind of roll, and her nails were long enamelled perfect things. She had a beautiful voice; when she said *Rosita* you could hear spice and heat. And when she said *Georgie* he could hear the tease, the lilt of confused accent, her laugh.

To snap Elsie out of his head, he stares at a *God grant me the serenity* . . . poster left tacked to the wall by Rose's last boyfriend, Paul, an earnest, dreamy kind of moron who liked to quote famous people George never heard of. He'd given George a biography his friend wrote about some explorer nobody gave a shit about. Unreadable. Although Rose rarely read much of anything, she could sound smart, but Paul left her anyway for a better version, another woman with dark hair, who was taller and had a degree. George never understood what attracted Paul to Rose in the first place; in fact, that's about what the guy told her right before they broke up: "I thought you were somebody else." Asshole.

Rose met these people at parties or something; it was beyond George how they would just move in.

She practically tore herself open for these men, showed them everything, made herself available, he guessed that's what it was called. If the guy needed some part of what he saw, he'd just take it. Leave Rose bleeding, sometimes real blood.

For days afterward, Rose would madly read her cards trying to figure out what was wrong with her. Instead, George thought, of seeing what was really going on at the time, what was black and white to George.

Trouble was, her cards were right about lots of things, but never anything that really mattered. She predicted a message coming from far away, and then got a phone call from a high-school friend who had moved to Chicago. The cards showed money. And she won fifty bucks from the Lotto 649, took George out for dinner. Right, that really changed her life.

Rose hears spirits in her yard. She goes out to the prairie and braids sweet grass and talks to Indian grandmothers. She gets visitations. Sometimes when George is over. Her eyes roll and she starts shaking like Dusky, and she says, "It's okay. It's just that little girl, the retarded one in the pinafore."

"What the hell does she want with you, Rose, tell her to get lost."

"She's lonely. Always so lonely."

Rose mostly gets visited when she's between men.

Rose claims there are moments when she can go invisible, but — haha — George has never seen it. He doesn't laugh when Rose talks about these things, because they are not for common knowledge, and she trusts George. But he remembers in San Francisco she hennaed her hair, like Elsie did, and even when he knew Rose wasn't there, George sometimes saw her peeking out from behind Elsie's skirts. So maybe it was true, about going invisible.

But Rose is never phoned or visited by Elsie, who Rose left curled up dead more than twenty years ago. Elsie first convulsing, then dying. *She wanted to, it was what she needed, I just helped her George, quit asking me all these questions.* George can only imagine. Can only imagine if she died the way Rose said. He sometimes wonders if she really died at all. She could have gone back to her grandfather's plantation in Brazil to lord over the mulattos, practise her Macumba, her weird voodoo. Or could have left little Rose for someone else, moved to New Orleans or Portugal.

Mostly he wonders if Elsie died because it was Rose who wanted her to. Because Rose wasn't able to leave her the way George finally had — suddenly, without warning — deciding if it wasn't that minute he might never leave at all; got on the bus, scared and polluted, promising himself that Rose would follow. But it wasn't for a year.

Elsie was an awfully quiet dead person, for a woman who supposedly grew up with weekly seances in her parents' dining room, who called on the dead herself, often. Awfully quiet. But George figures that's how the dead should be.

Rose is looking at him. "Go home, you're tired. You aren't talking, go home."

"Ya, okay." He kisses Rose's cheek, which smells of smoke and patchouli oil. Brushes through the spirits in her yard, and drives home on the main highway. He won't cut his hair too short, it's thick and wavy like Rose's, and in dim light he can look like her, like a woman.

He floats in Elsie's clawfooted tub; she washes him all over, gently, "You're pretty as a girl, Georgie," and the part of him that escapes the storm in his head is perched up on a shelf, next to the loofah and bath oil, watching, wondering how he came to be there, in this place with this woman, with Elsie who strokes him as she shaves his legs, dries him off, dresses him in her long silk robe.

She would be almost an old woman now.

She asked me to help her die, quit saying all this to me Georgie, it was nothing, she just needed to die. But he thinks of how Elsie liked to bring the dead with her into rooms, watch the chills run around the skin of her living guests. The books she showed Rosita and George, people coupled in impossible ways.

He gets home at twenty to one, hears Dusky barking in the house at the sound of his truck. Lets her out for a pee. Drinks beer from a bottle and feels his lips swell.

The phone rings in his sleep. He knows it is a dream, because his mother is calling. He answers anyway and strains to hear her distant voice, thinks he should be telling her things, but doesn't know what and it pains him. He says phone again, I'm tired now, and her voice fades away. Changes his mind, wants to hear her some more, but can't.

He thinks about his mother phoning in his dream, has no idea if she said anything. He makes it up.

Georgie, do you have some money

I'm fine Mom

Did you put away the ironing board

I put everything away, it's all cleaned up

Are you keeping your sister out of trouble

Yes

Did you find some lunch

Yes

I love you, Georgie

I love you, Mom, and so does Rosie

But he wonders if that is a lie.

He doesn't tell Rose about these phone calls. She already has enough company, and he doesn't want her trying any of her tricks.

FOR A BOY

THE MAGPIE FEATHERS LIE IN A SCATTERY HEAP as if they'd been torn from an old-fashioned hat — slender and long, iridescent over their black — and the boy thinks how lovely they are even in their slaughter. A patch of thistle blossoms has burst dry, their whitish globes of down are thick enough almost to bury the last cut of wheat, and these blossoms hold the feathers high on the swath.

The swath, with its feathers, stops at the edge of a little-used road, a north-south trail intersecting cropped fields of canola and spring wheat and yellow peas. Along this road, early evening, the boy walks back toward the grain truck, hoping, as he always has, that his father will not be waiting and angry.

A long time ago, his mother had taught him this, which she called "The Magpie Song" although they never sang it, but chanted:

> *One for sorrow*
> *Two for joy*
> *Three for a girl*
> *Four for a boy*

One for sorrow, that's how he generally spotted the magpies, as solitary birds. But when he did see one, he tried to pretend he hadn't noticed, at least not until he could find the second. Almost always there was only one, and he thought for a long time it wasn't fair, but the more summers that went by he decided it had nothing at all to do with fair, but just there's lots more sorrow flying around people's heads than there is joy. It isn't as if the magpies are causing it, just they are telling you how they know sorrow is there.

He is surprised, though, to see the feathers this evening. It's a tough game to catch a magpie. A real tough game. His dog never could, as far as the boy knew, and it made the dog wild when the magpies stole kibble from the dish and strutted and swore at him in bird-talk, always just out of reach. And he was fast, his dog Blue, a Chesapeake, a big liver-lipped yellow-eyed mahogany-coated waterproof monster who went out to hunt with the boy's dad sometimes, but his dad wasn't really much of a hunter and never trained Blue, mostly just gave him shit.

What animal had got that magpie? he wonders. And left no bones, just the pretty feathers held high on those thistles. His dad would be mad to see the cropped thistles so heavy on the edge of the field like that. Every year, he said, there were more of them and it didn't matter how much chemical you used.

Tomorrow will be the harvest moon, and his favourite walk along that north-south trail.

He doesn't get to do it every year, not if the crops are heavy. When that happens he can't leave the truck for more than a couple of minutes, and often not at all, but follows the combine in the field until he's loaded up, then rushes to the bins and backs up and augers, and lowers the hoist even as he's driving out of the yard and back to the combine. He doesn't tell his dad he drives with the hoist coming down, though.

Whenever he walks down that trail in the evening of the first harvest moon, he sees the world is split in two. To his right is the west, as it always is on the way back to the truck. And the sun there, skimming over the horizon on its path toward the north. When he was in fifth grade he wrote a paragraph for his teacher and said how much he loved it when the sun set in the north. His paragraph was given back to him marked with a red *X*. It sets in the west, she had said, and he tried to explain how it didn't really but she got tired of talking with him about it and told him he had better pay attention and because he was a farm boy he *really* better had.

He didn't drive the big truck then, not until he was fourteen would his dad let him, and then only because his mother was too sick and tired, and the boy's legs ached they'd grown so fast the previous year and he could reach the clutch easily.

He watched carefully, paying better attention every year. And every year the sun set almost in the north. The world is not square, although it is measured as such by some teachers. But that trail did split the world in two at certain times of the year. Tomorrow would be one of those times. And for a few days afterwards it would almost do the same, but not quite, because it seemed the moon took a longer course. He will walk south toward the truck with the sun rolling slow and falling toward the north, and as it rolls it sometimes swells until the edges become soft and blazing and the clouds are no longer clouds but great long masses of purple and bronze and gold, shifting and soaking in the reflected night as they, too, travel with the sun into the north.

And to his left is the curve of the east, where night has already arrived as a particular blue which deepens even as he watches, it deepens as he walks south toward the truck and searches for the harvest moon. It will come like a great egg hatched from the space between earth and sky. It will come as a thin, bright stroke which begins to bulge upward, pulling itself so carefully into itself, pulling away from the earth, as if the earth is laying an egg upside down, appearing as part circle, to bulging half, to full, and there it rests on the horizon for a moment, not round at all but fat and soft and elliptical. A line will appear under it suddenly, and that is the moment it has broken free of the earth and it floats up into the night, and as it rises it shapes itself into a perfect round and becomes harder and brighter, forcing the deep blue into the black-blue of night.

That is how the world is split in two. Even as he follows the moon, he follows the sun at his right, where beyond the blaze and the colours are hills to the west, still bright with the dust rising from them, a band of green, a band of quiet yellow, where it is still the day.

This year he is eighteen and the crops are sparse and weed filled. Tomorrow he will see the world split in two.

Blue would come out to the field with him if he could, but he has been put in the habit of remaining in the yard to watch the house. In the house had lain the boy's mother, only now she was gone. They had all believed she would die. For almost three years they believed that, but she lost a breast and part of the muscle above that, and then, too tired to listen to the boy and his father, she left.

She had told the boy it was his father who caused her illness. His father told him it was her bitter bones that had brought it on.

Blue had adored the boy's mother. She was the one who spent hours some days, running her hands over Blue's slightly wiry, slightly oily, coat as he lay on the deck. She pulled his velvet ears between her fingers and took each leg and massaged, lapping the movements of her strong hands right down to the huge paw, created wide for swimming, where she would rub between the pads and pull carefully on his toes until his eyes were almost rolled back into his head from bliss. She would turn him completely on his back and then his legs would fall away and outward and his mouth would lax, showing parts of his white teeth. Then he looked like a cat, an almost-smiling, hypnotized cat. She had done all of this, she said, to gentle him because Chesapeakes are a rough dog. But the boy knew that more than anything, she did it to gentle herself.

Blue had cried harder than any of them when she left and the boy wanted to take him into the house, but his father would have nothing of it. Blue had searched the abandoned vegetable garden every day until the snow became too deep to hold any hope, and although it has been a year now, he still watches for the boy's mother to come out the kitchen door in the morning.

Blue always walks to the bins to watch him unload, but the boy usually has time for no more than a quick rub on his head, and Blue will sigh and go back to the yard to wait.

The boy tries to think about his mother, how she really was, how they all really were together. He knows she was not happy. Was she always not happy? He knows she liked him well enough, and joked with him more than she ever did with his father, but even her humour sometimes had a meanness to it, and came to the very edge of insulting a person. Especially his father. Bitter boned, he'd said. As if that were a medical condition. Never enough for her, never satisfied, never should have married her in the first place, never belonged, never tried to belong, never went out of her way to be nice to people.

She *did so* try, the boy had said. She always tried, she invited people to eat with them if they dropped by, she *was so* nice. But as he'd said it, although he knew everything about her feeding people was true, he understood, beyond that, his mother was not a usual person and the concept of nice was a complicated one for her. He remembers seeing her, her mouth set tight as she made the coffee and hauled out some baking, and often there had been a puzzled kind of look to her, as if she might start to cry and was fighting it. And very often, after the people left, she would ask the boy how had the meal or the cake *really* tasted, and she would ask him in a few different ways. But was it too spicy, soggy, dry, bland? She could cook better than almost anybody he'd ever known, but she worried more about it too. She even worried when she fed someone he knew she didn't like too well.

It was right for her to have gone, he thinks. It was right for her to go away. Maybe soon she will find a place which will not puzzle her, and will sweeten her bones. He hopes she gets another dog, maybe smaller than Blue, but a strong dog who likes cities.

The boy tries to think about his father, how he really is, how they all really were together. He believes his father is not happy either, but what does happy really mean, and was he happier after his wife left even though he'd cried? Would it have been happier for them if the boy's mother had died after all and they could have a real excuse not to be happy? The boy wonders about his father, who he will see anyway in a few minutes, and decides he will look carefully at him and possibly ask him. Then he decides he will say nothing at all, because he has already asked the question in different ways many times before and it's either: sure I'm happy, or what the hell is there to be happy about? or what's happy got to do with anything?

The word "happy" is ping-ponging so much in his head that the boy stops on the trail. He breathes in the cooling air, very slowly, and lets it out very slowly. He looks to his feet, at his boots with the laces loose and their ends tucked in, and there beside his feet at two black crickets in the dust of the road, chirruping as they do with the noise of a thumb being run along the edge of a comb.

Tomorrow the world will split in two and he will see it happen, and then he will leave.

Blue would come with him if he could, but he has been put in the habit of remaining in the yard to watch the house. In the house there will be nobody then, except his father at night. Blue wouldn't be happy if the boy took him away from his yard. And his father, though he knows the boy will be gone by the end of tomorrow, will be angry if the combine is left waiting tonight for the truck, and for the boy to drive it a last time.

EMERALD AND ANGUS

EMERALD AND HER HALF-BROTHER ANGUS moved into the town of Pinkerton one day, virtually unannounced.

The only person who expected them was the sister-in-law of an old widower who died the previous winter, and it was she who'd placed the advertisement for his one and a half storey house in a farming weekly. This paper was read widely across the Canadian west. Emerald was not at all from the Canadian west, but had lived first in northern Ontario and from there, moved with her mother to more American states than her mother could name, then back to Canada.

She discovered the farming paper in a Vancouver bookshop, enticed by its huge banner headline which read: *The Crow is Dead.*

She did not count herself an especially superstitious person, and felt closer to the main than the fringe, but she did believe a crow was somehow a special bird. It seemed to feature pretty heavily in some native mythologies, although she didn't know why, and when crows became a nuisance and the guns and poison were brought out, they seemed impossible to kill. Crows and ravens both, she'd heard, had been known to lead predators to vulnerable animals by circling and making a lot of noise above the prey, so that afterwards they could share the proceeds.

Emerald kept her own crow a secret. What was the point in telling, and who would she tell, about the Sunday morning a crow tapped on the seventh-floor bedroom window to wake her and say in unmistakable English, "your mother has died." Emerald said to it, "what the hell are you talking about?" and leapt out of bed. The crow flew away, and Emerald frantically tracked down her mother at a hotel in London, which was nine hours ahead of them, and then had a brief and awkward conversation with her. She mentioned nothing about birds. That evening, (London time), her mother, and mother's gentleman friend, stepped out into traffic to hail a cab, when they were both struck dead by a courier van which was hit from behind by a cement lorry whose brakes had failed.

The one aspect of all of this which really bothered Emerald was why her mother's death was announced prematurely.

The Crow is dead. What could that possibly mean; how should she take this — with relief, as a trick, a warning of preventable tragedy? She scanned the lead article for something of significance, but was disappointed to find it was nothing but politics and trains. Money, money, money, discussed endlessly by men in suits, the kind of self-important guys her mother went for and had twice married. But she bought the paper and took it back to the apartment she and Angus rented for the year. She went through the personal classifieds, poultry, working dogs, horses various, ratites (emus and ostriches), business opportunities (bakery, general store, gas stop, outfitter). And then, under properties for sale she found *Country living in*

Pinkerton, a convenient town setting far from heavy industry, close to city and amenities.

Far from heavy industry. It seemed an unusual, but intriguing, phrase to include in a house ad. Far from pulp mills, eight lane freeways, nuclear power plants, auto factories. Possibly light and industrious people would live there, the kind she most enjoyed casual friendships with. The thought of owning a house after so many transient years had its own appeal, and as a result she made inquiries and accomplished the entire deal unseen and by telephone. It was arranged that the sister-in-law was not going to be there at all, since she lived almost a hundred miles from the town, and she instructed Emerald with an elaborate set of directions involving paths and shrubs and exactly a count of five clay pots next to one of the two sheds in which would be the house-key under a varnish brush. Any problems just go to the town office.

Angus had cried and threatened a tantrum when his sister told him they would once again be moving, but she said, "Stop this minute or I swear I'll change your name to Corvid." Angus was twenty-five at the time, round as a toddler and almost ten years younger than herself. He took the threat seriously. At eighteen she'd changed her own name from Doreen, and had refused from then on to answer to anything but Emerald, from him or anybody else.

Angus had come to live with Emerald long before their mother's accident. In fact, Angus's late father, the elderly Alec MacPhee, had left a good part of his estate to this awkward, mostly unemployable son, but the money was entrusted to his stepdaughter Doreen, aka Emerald. The better part of Alec MacPhee's estate went to his wife, who then not only possessed the better parts of two marriages, but was relieved of responsibility for both her pudgy, silly boy and her stuffy husband.

Emerald and Angus did fine and lived well under the trust fund. After a crow possibly first alerted Emerald, and then directed the cement lorry and courier van to the whereabouts of their vulnerable mother, they lived even better.

She and Angus loaded her new Westfalia, travelling light as they always did, and drove east for three days.

Throughout her adult life, Emerald had enough means that she should never have to take a real job, but she usually did anyway. She often found work for Angus as well, but for him it had to be a short-term situation where he was able to keep his focus long enough to finish. The late elderly Alec MacPhee had been so overjoyed with the birth of this, his only, child he was quite blind to most of the obvious limitations and downright faults that Angus possessed. He believed that Angus would never have belonged in a sheltered workshop, for instance, which was the sort of thing professionals had recommended his father provide for him. Alec MacPhee was enraged and insulted by what he viewed as medical prejudice and flawed tests. He hired a succession of tutors over the years, but the most they accomplished with Angus's tantrums and uncertain intelligence was drumming into him the importance of baths and clean clothes. As a result, he always looked very neat.

Angus loved to shop for clothes. In fact he loved to shop for everything, which was the one great benefit to the frequent moves he and Emerald made; whenever they arrived at a new home they had to replace all of those things they had rid themselves of before they left — kitchenware, toiletries, furniture, towels, sometimes a cat. This passion of his made things difficult for Emerald. Even though she'd gotten angry with him over and over, and pleaded for him to wait until she got home, sometimes Angus went shopping without her. Being Angus, he had no real idea of how things were paid for.

Emerald had hoped that the lack of heavy industry surrounding their new home included lack of access to malls and department stores. On the highway, as they approached Pinkerton for the first time, it became clear that the town included a lack of almost everything and she began to laugh. She laughed hard enough it woke up Angus.

It was early afternoon, toward the end of April, and record-breaking hot when they drove up and down the streets until they found a house that fit the sister-in-law's description. It sat up on a low embankment, far back from the street, almost completely surrounded by an overgrown caragana hedge. Cement steps, flanked by stone, were set into a rise leading to the front porch.

Angus said, "I don't like this much," and grumbled as he followed Emerald round to the yard, where they found the two sheds, one with five empty clay pots next to it, and from there the house-key under a hardened varnish brush.

There was something comforting to Emerald about once again walking into an unfamiliar place that would soon become her own, opening windows, looking in cupboards, working out which room was to be used for what, breathing in the subtle traces of someone else's past.

Sometimes the odour was only the hint of a person who'd been there a few months, and the echoes of the others before that one, people like Emerald who didn't need to stay overlong, who were just passing through or found something more interesting to leave for. This house was strangely silent, perhaps, she thought, because it had kept only one family, now long gone.

Having nothing to sleep on, they didn't spend the first night there after unloading the van but drove to the city, almost an hour away, to spend the next day selecting furniture and other goods to be trucked out.

Pinkerton was not like any other place she'd lived but she took it all in stride, the smaller sounds of a small town, a sudden squabble of nesting birds, the greetings — which ranged from a cautious nod to extensive interviews — given her by almost every person she met on the street.

Some of them took in her details as they talked, in order to pass them along. Her thick silver bracelets, pedicured feet, black jeans and men's dress shirt opened over a camisole or T-shirt, frizzy blonde hair, long and tied back, *probably dyed. Seemed nice enough, sounded sort-of American. Funny brother, kind of simple. Not sure what she does for a living, didn't really come out with it.*

Emerald quickly learned to say "between jobs, mainly office administration" and allude to interviews, supposing that to be recognised as independently well-off would gain less respect around there than if she were someone on pogey.

After getting some advice, plus bedding plants and sprinklers, from the people who ran the ranch and feed store, she put Angus to work cleaning up flower beds and working a tiller through the old vegetable garden, which she'd decided would revert to lawn. Angus was also the main floor washer and putter away of laundry, but that only went so far in a day. She taped up notices which offered his services for lawn-mowing, raking, and general yard work. His first call was to fill in for a week at the greenhouse a few miles from town, where Emerald delivered him at seven o'clock the next morning. At noon, the owner phoned Emerald and asked her to come get her brother, that he couldn't tell one damned plant from the next and kept coming to the house for water or the bathroom or something to eat, and besides he was scared of their dog.

The next week, an afternoon when she thought Angus was still trimming a hedge down the street, she walked into the Co-op store and found the counter heaped with boxes of crackers, playing cards, chocolate milk and other things already bagged, and Angus there arguing with a young girl behind the till.

He picked up a can of asparagus and pushed it in front of the girl's face. "J-j-just who the hell do you th-think, th-think you are. M-my, m-my can pay for this. J-j-just who the hell do you th-think you are."

His voice was pitched high as he stuttered, which meant he was almost in full-blown temper. Even as Emerald rushed toward him, the woman in line behind Angus tapped his shoulder and said sternly, "Now that is quite enough of that, you hear, that is quite enough of that."

He whirled around to her, spittle bubbling from the corners of his mouth, and the empty hand flailing toward her nose.

"M-my, m-my, m-my."

Emerald said very loudly, "Excuse me."

Angus turned from the woman, red-faced. "M-my, m-my can pay for it."

"No, Angus. You can't." Emerald looked to the girl, who stood there with a shaky smile, and tears starting from pale eyes.

"M-my."

"'*I'* nothing. You can't pay for this without me and you know you can't. Look at this poor little girl here, you scared her half to death."

"Didn't." He pouted and shoved his hands into his pockets, muttering.

Emerald walked past him and pushed aside everything he had tried to buy, telling the woman in line to please go ahead.

"I'm sorry," said the girl. "I *give* him the total but he didn't have a card or nothing. I'm sorry."

Emerald spent the next few months with something like a sense of adventure, painting and decorating, arranging to have new sidewalks poured, settling herself and Angus into the house and the town as well as she knew how. She felt as if this could easily become a permanent place for them, and had already been theirs for a long time. There were catalogues strewn about the kitchen for things she'd never had a possible use for until then, such as airtight wood stoves, herbaceous perennials, Japanese gardening tools. In the past, if a balcony or small patio came with their apartment, she might look for old teapots or jardinières at yard sales, and pack them with annual flowers, but what she was accomplishing in Pinkerton operated on a whole new scale.

With the variety of work Emerald gave him, Angus's grumbling toned down over the summer, but his moment of true satisfaction was watching seventy-year-old Cliff, one of their neighbours, nail together the boxed and curved forms of the new sidewalk, and mix gravel and water and pour the thick cement. He was entranced by each tiny procedure as it led to the next, and took note of the creased tool pouch Cliff reached into without looking and how he pulled out the right sized nail every time, the chalky scabs of cement dried on overalls or skin, and his cracked and blackened thumbnail. There had been many opportunities for Angus to stop and watch men at work before this — something was always being built in cities — but almost all had quickly ended with him being made fun of, or cursed at and sent away, or with a policeman herding him off. Pinkerton was different and so was Cliff.

Cliff talked as he worked, a little to himself sometimes, but quite a lot if Angus was around. He explained everything he was doing as he did it, and if he'd explained it enough times then he told Angus about people he knew and what they were up to. Angus would sometimes run into the house and say things to Emerald like: "Can you believe those sonsabitches sold Cliff's truck he just sold them and they sold it for more money, can you believe that?" And she'd say, "Which sonsabitches are you talking about, Angus?" Every time he'd run back out to ask for more information, and Emerald would hear Cliff laugh.

She thought it was a good thing, to hear a man laugh in her own backyard.

Emerald liked to believe she didn't think about men too much, and had kept most relationships she ever allowed to develop, short. There was the presence of Angus, of course, which gave her almost as much responsibility as would having a child, but he presented a more daunting, maybe disturbing prospect to any man she brought home. Life without her brother was never an option, but life with most men, according to what she'd seen of her own surrogate fathers and her mother's love life, was pretty lame. Only the elderly Alec MacPhee had won her heart, and that because he really had no idea at all about children, and spent a lot more money than time on her, and the time he did spend was kind and cautious and excruciatingly polite. For Emerald's mother, he had clearly been the biggest bore on earth.

Cliff had a son, whom Emerald had only glimpsed once in the summer when he stopped by her yard to pass a message on to his father. She was standing at the kitchen sink at the time, and suddenly found herself embarrassed by that, as if he'd assume kitchen sinks were her usual place to be, and backed away from the window so as not to be seen. But she thought the son had glanced her way. The brief image she had of him didn't tell her enough, she knew, to justify her questioning and mulling over it the way she did; they hadn't even met, there was nothing for her to work on but imagination. His name was Gord, Cliff told her that day. She saw it as a clipped, got-stuff-to-do sort of name, straightforward like his father's. He was thirty-six, and divorced, and he worked the rigs quite often when carpentry slowed down. Both were jobs which might contribute to Cliff's son's outstanding build, or maybe he just came by it naturally. Emerald decided there was far too much time on her hands if fantasies over unknown country boys named Gord were starting to invade. Even classic chisel-jawed, dark-haired country boys.

She made some calls to acquaintances and friends to help her out. The city had amenities, as the sister-in-law had advertised, and in September she began an office job there with a small movie company.

By then, after five months in town, Angus was beginning to feel his away around. When they lived in Vancouver he'd had a couple of coffee haunts where he was well known and visited almost daily, and Emerald could usually trust he would stay out of trouble. Pinkerton had two cafés and Angus had already made himself at home in both. His favourite was at the highway, where he sometimes spent entire days watching traffic go by, studying everything that pulled off the road and fuelled up, getting into conversations. On his own efforts, for the first time in his life, he got offers for small jobs.

"I need a cap," he said to Emerald.

"For?"

"I need a cap for *work* so l-let's, let's go to the Co-op."

The only caps sold at the Co-op said "Co-op" and Angus picked out one red, one blue. She also took him to town and bought him work gloves and thick socks and heavy brown canvas overalls with a matching jacket, and good steel-toed boots. After that, the only time he wasn't wearing those boots, he was sleeping, and the boots were right beside him.

Angus dug some holes for other people's new trees; he discovered there was something in the world called a block and tackle and was allowed to use it a couple of times to stretch barbed wire; once he helped mix and spread cement with Cliff, and after that, several times with Gord.

"I helped Gord for six hours," he told Emerald when she'd gotten home from work. "Six hours and I sweated like a sonofabitch and I cut my hand so good it bled right into the cement barrow and Gord he just laughed and mixed her right in."

He showed her the left hand, which had been sliced quite deeply on the inside fleshy pad by his thumb, the wound now dry and black.

"What's with the 'sonofabitch' every time you open your mouth, Angus?"

"You don't get mad when Cliff says it."

"Cliff isn't my brother and neither is Gord."

Angus gave her a sly look, as if he knew he was going to say something provoking. "Gord thinks you're pretty."

Emerald was appalled at how pleased that made her, and considered maybe it was time to move again. She said, "It's really good that you worked six hours, Angus. That's a hard day."

Gord didn't waste much time after Angus's announcement regarding Emerald, but showed up at the back door the next weekend, without warning. He knocked and grinned hard at Emerald when she swung open the door.

"I guess we never got formally introduced," he said, and stuck out his hand.

Once again Emerald had been at the kitchen sink, and making what she saw as a deception even worse, was barefoot and without makeup. At least, she thought, there were no biscuits in the oven, and the radio in her kitchen was tuned in to the classical, not country, station.

Cowboys, good ol' boys, weather-roughened country boys, salt of the earth hockey-playing whoop-it-uppers, streamed like a song in her head as she shook hands with Cliff 's son and considered him. She invited him in for coffee.

Gord stared at the radio and said, "I like this stuff. Cliff says I'm like the darkies 'cause I like to work to music, especially opera, something relaxing about it. Got lots of opera."

Emerald deliberated saying something about "darkies", but that had been Cliff's word, not Gord's.

"I work to music as well. But never opera. I think it's the kind of thing you either love or hate."

"You're right about that one," said Gord. "Makes most people scream and run for the first exit to hear opera, but it's like a drug with me, no other word for it."

Before this, if Emerald had seen Gord walking down the street toward her, or coming into a restaurant where she was with friends, the second glance she might have given him would be an admiring one, but the idea of forming a romance with him would have been a joke. Worn jeans, working hands.

But here, in Pinkerton's quiet autumn, in this kitchen with crabapple trees outside the window and her own flower beds waiting for the next year, stood a man who had first made friends with Angus.

Soon after this visit Gord hurt his back at work, so he said, and was on compensation. Angus delighted in Gord's ever more frequent visits, and the extra jobs Gord found for him and helped him with around the house. Emerald would often come home from the city to find Gord there, busy with Angus by his side, at first at work in the yard, clearing debris in the back, pruning trees, replacing the hinges on the old gate; but after a while, when winter set in, Gord was in their house. It had never been usual for Angus to have people over. In this place lots of rules had changed, she reasoned, people dropped by, people talked to strangers, people gave each other a hand. And Gord would be restless and bored without a regular job, and would appreciate having things to do around there.

It was a Saturday in November when Gord sent Angus down to the store with a long list and some money. The second Angus was out the door, he grabbed Emerald into her room, where they made fast, hard love, and then again, taking their time.

From the moment Gord took hold of her and pulled her onto the bed, Emerald felt unreal and dizzy, that she somehow had no control over this scene, it was a romance-novel plundering, which had begun as almost a rape. And true to the genre, afterwards it seemed they had become a couple.

For the first time she thought she understood her own mother, and how it was she had allowed and even welcomed the invasion of a man.

She began looking forward to his company at evening meals, and to their passion, which had to wait for the absence of her brother. They went to local dances together, sometimes to the hotel bar and, as with any new job, she learned the kind of banter and skimming gossip needed to mark her as less an outsider. He offered to build a deck for her, come spring, and a gazebo.

It was never love, for Emerald. It might have been and she wished it were, but she was very careful not to use the word with Gord.

He thought they were perfect, he and Emerald and Angus, that all of the right events had converged and brought them together, everything was part of a divine plan, from the ad in the farming paper that had drawn her there, her needing a new sidewalk, his bad back, even the fact that neither of them had living mothers. It was all meant to be, as they were meant to be. He could not understand why Emerald didn't want him to move in with them, even though Angus clearly thought the world of him.

One night Emerald woke up from a dream, rigid and afraid in the dark of her bedroom. She'd been crossing the highway, she and Angus, and in the dream the road wasn't flat, but rolling and steep. She hadn't seen what had knocked them down and left them, maybe dead, on the edge of the road. That was her dream. But in the darkness her fear had created a shadow in the room, and the shadow moved and then spoke. It whispered, "Hi sweetheart." In her relief she moved over in the bed and pulled Gord toward her. "Don't *do* that, you scared the hell out of me, please don't ever do that again." But he did it quite a few times after that.

That spring she seemed to find extra things to do in the city, and volunteered to make calls and put up posters for an actor she'd met who had just finished recording her first CD. She often didn't get home until late evening. Angus had never minded when Emerald was gone at mealtimes, she always arranged accounts for him with the local restaurants, but Gord didn't like it all. "At least commit your weekends," he'd said. She said she would try.

"Gord says why are you ignoring him so much."

"Angus, I think the man knows how to talk, he doesn't need your two cents worth."

"M-my, m-my think you should marry Gord then he could live here."

She asked Gord to please not discuss their relationship with her brother, that he had a very simple view of things and if he wanted to say something he should say it to her. To which Gord asked her to marry him.

It was, for Emerald, an unforgivable question. She put a stop to Gord completely.

Angus was impossible after they broke up; he phoned Gord constantly and often met him at the highway café, reporting Gord's sadness back to his sister. He cried because Gord told him they weren't allowed to work together anymore since Emerald wouldn't allow it, a lie which made Emerald completely convinced she was right to end it.

Soon afterwards, Cliff reported that his son's back was healed and he was leaving for the rigs. "You hear what I'm telling you, Emerald. He's gone six weeks and it wouldn't kill you to talk to the man before he goes, he's been nothing but good to you."

"I'm sorry Cliff, it's just not going to happen. Maybe when he gets back. But listen, if you can get Angus busy at something special, I would really appreciate that, he's taking it pretty hard."

"If that boy's grieving then he's got more sense than you do."

It was very strange to her for an ex-lover's parent to intercede as Cliff had, but maybe it was the way things were done around there, another bit of culture she hadn't known of.

A rocky beginning to their life in Pinkerton, that's what all of this amounted to, and she decided that Angus would have to start learning to cope with some of it himself. Meanwhile Emerald filled the clay pots and the flower beds, took Angus for a weekend in Calgary, and generally worked very hard. She did think of Gord, and more often than she wanted to. She missed his strong hands on her body, his sureness with tools, the firm but humouring way he had with Angus; she missed his easy laugh, and his company which had bought her instant access to much of the town. She'd gone only once to the bar without him, afterward, and got casual nods or "how's it going?", but no invitation from the same people she and Gord had sat and got a little drunk with a few times. That casual companionship was gone with him gone.

It was late July, a still and perfect evening, cooling gently from the day under a velvet Rousseau sky with a crescent moon. Emerald was a block from the general store carrying home a bag of milk and soft brown bread, a chocolate bar for Angus and salty cheese snacks for herself, when a Jeep Cherokee rolled quietly up beside her, so quiet and slow she knew that it had to be Gord.

She took a deep breath and hugged the bag to her chest, turning toward him. He had stopped, with the motor running; the window on the passenger side was down and he moved over to talk with her. *He is a handsome man.* That is what Emerald thought as they looked at one another, *he is a handsome, pathetic case of a man.*

"I'll drive you home," he said.

"I'm sorry, Gord."

"What're you sorry for?"

"Everything. It would never have worked, you know that, but I'm sorry."

Gord lifted his head a little higher, tilting it slightly, and stared up and past Emerald toward the sky. His eyes tightened at the corners, as if tears were forced back.

"We need to talk. Please." He said it so quietly and with such sadness.

119

He looked at her then, and opened the passenger door. "Please," he said again. He moved over for her and patted the seat, and Emerald got in beside him and closed the door.

Gord drove slowly at first, and said very little except that he was trying to collect his thoughts. Emerald was quiet as well, lulled by the stillness of the night and the sense of Gord's mourning, the familiar smell of him. They cruised along the near-empty streets of Pinkerton, past darkening bird baths and garden gnomes, toward the edge of town.

The Jeep's door locks clicked shut. Emerald bit her lip, and carefully reached over and tried her lock, and then the window.

"Won't work, but don't be scared, I just need to make sure you'll talk to me."

"Stop. Right now, Gord. Stop and let me out." She tried to keep her voice steady, there was nothing gained by letting him see he'd gotten to her, all she needed to do was say something.

"We'll go, we'll go . . . to see Cliff, okay, we'll talk this over with Cliff."

He floored the Jeep and Emerald started yelling for him to stop, but it was coming out like screams. She pushed the grocery bag at him, stupidly she knew, and he grabbed it and swung it into her face. The carton of milk hit the bridge of her nose and her eyes watered. There was nothing steady left in her. She pulled herself in front of him, looking for something to free her, the master lock, window controls, something, but found the horn and pushed hard. Gord kept his left hand on the wheel and took her by the hair, twisting it and forcing her off. He said, "Quit it."

He drove fast, straight north for a few minutes, then took a sharp left down a grid. The sky was a deeper, luminous blue and the crescent moon had risen higher; brush appeared on either side of them, gradually thickening and blackening. Emerald tried to keep track of directions, and distances, the feel of gravel under the Jeep giving way to sand. So she could tell somebody where he took her. Who would she tell? Once again they turned north, but the track wound so much that only the moon, when it showed sometimes above the bluffs, was constant. Then he stopped, opened his window, turned off the Jeep, leaned back and put the keys deep in his jeans pocket.

Emerald listened very hard. Nothing. No dog's bark, no rumbling from the grid they'd left far behind, only Gord's breathing, and then a slight wind giving voice to the tops of poplars. He had brought her, deliberately, to nowhere.

He reached over and she stiffened, but he only took her grocery bag and threw it out his window.

Emerald began to sob.

Gord looked at her, as if he was puzzled. "What's the matter with you?"

"You can't throw that out. It's Angus's chocolate, I promised him I'd get it, you can't throw that out."

"Shit. All right." He opened the door wide and strode toward the bag.

Maybe her door would open now but she didn't have time to find out, she scrambled out after him and away from the Jeep and began to run. She could not make herself quit sobbing, it was blinding her and stealing her breath, and the soft sand dragged at her feet. She veered toward the poplars which, she could now see, were thin and sparse and even in the dark would not hide her for long. But none of it mattered because Gord tackled her before she could leave the track, bringing her down heavy on one side, and he had her by the shoulders and banged her head into the dirt, again and again.

"Sick bastard." She didn't know she'd said it aloud, but Gord must have heard because he slapped her across the mouth. Emerald turned her head to one side so she didn't have to look at him, and so he couldn't see her eyes. There was a tree root growing up out of the road, right there beside her, and she wondered if it belonged to one of those spindly poplars, struggling to create their little forest in all this sand; and she looked up, blinking away the last of her tears, and past Gord's head, searching for the bright Rousseau moon. There it was. He hit her mouth again, and she thought she heard her teeth crackle. Blood began to fill her throat, and she turned her head and spat.

She whispered, to the ground, "Cut it out, Gord."

He got off her and stood. Emerald looked up at him, dark and tall over her, his strong hands hanging at his sides, tears already dirty down his cheeks. He said, "Fine."

She sat up very slowly, still not knowing if it was safe to talk. She would be careful and polite, like the elderly Alec MacPhee. "Take me home to Angus now, would you please Gord."

"I'll take you to Cliff, and you can just explain to him why I'm going to end up in jail, you snobby little slut."

"You aren't going to jail, I won't say anything. Would you please get Angus's chocolate for me, and then let's go home."

He reached down a hand and yanked her to her feet. He said, "This is the deal. You don't touch me, you don't talk to me, you don't say shit until we get to Cliff's, and then you can tell him what you did to me." He thumped where he figured his heart should be.

"Okay, Gord."

He walked ahead of her, quickly. Almost every part of her began to hurt, and she wondered, as she struggled to keep up with him, what exactly had caused some of these pains. She could see him bending and gathering not just the chocolate, but everything she had bought. The bread would be wrecked.

Maybe she'd fallen asleep. Emerald almost remembered getting into the Jeep, but they were in front of Cliff's house, her with the grocery bag and Gord practically shoving her along the walk, and muttering. Cliff opened the door. He said to Gord, "Give me your keys, Son, and get into the house."

Emerald could hardly walk back to the Jeep. She needed to lie on Cliff's lawn; she needed a lot of sleep and then a hot bath. Cliff said not a word to her, but drove her to the house up on the embankment, leaned over and opened her door. She went into the house alone.

It was a few days before Emerald could begin to arrange everything, a few days for the dizziness to go away and her to decide that no teeth had been broken. Her cheeks and jaw were badly bruised, as was most of one side of her entire body, but the raw split in her lip was healing and shouldn't leave a scar. Angus cried a lot and made her tea or soup, and offered many times to kill Gord. She said he wasn't worth it.

"Where should we go, Angus, where would you like to live?"

"Vancouver. And that restaurant where everybody brings their dogs, okay?"

"Okay."

ANDREA'S KITCHEN

ANDREA WAS ONE OF THOSE VERY LOVELY GIRLS who, at a very early age, was long in the leg, full enough in the lips and breast, and so casual in the way she walked that the men whose heads she turned mistook her for a full-blown woman, and boys, who such girls never bother with, were so caught off guard they lost their breath. These girls do exist, and they are rarely stupid, but have the goods to hold up decent, non-giggling conversation with much older and better-educated men, men who delight in whatever they might say, and whose eyes also soak in that absolute fineness and luminescence of skin, which although not beauty in itself, is a brief-lived miracle. Men are drawn like flies to the pitcher plant, and for moments their only wish is to be consumed.

Andrea was seventeen and had been waiting tables for over a year when she first saw Mark. She'd been working the past while at a frenetic, black-tiled, music-dense restaurant, with chalk menus on the walls and Mexican cuisine. He came in looking expensive and sexy, acne-scorched face and carefully cut hair to the shoulders, a lanky young guy's build to him although she could tell he was pushing thirty.

It wasn't that he said anything special to her at the time, men had been saying such things since she was barely in high school, but he seemed like a lot more fun than the rest.

After a couple of months Mark told her to move in with him and she couldn't see why not. Andrea had long accepted that most events have the same weight as the ones that came before.

She packed up what she owned, which wasn't much of anything, said goodbye to her boisterous small town room-mate, and moved across the city to a condo furnished with leather and teak and a stainless steel designer kitchen with a food processor and reefers in a Japanese bowl.

Mark did business out of a succession of beat-up Mercedes, and as time went on it seemed that more and more of what he was supposed to sell went up his nose, at least enough that she made sure to keep working and have cash of her own.

He had a dressmaker renovate his jeans with long zippers that went way under him, so Andrea would have easier access. And although she thought she'd already known how to do this as well, he taught her to cook.

This was what Mark told Andrea on the two occasions of her two abortions: *But baby you know I have to plant my seed.*

She didn't think it was meant as consolation or even explanation.

Of all their parties and times together, it was the only thing she finally couldn't make enough sense of.

When Andrea was nineteen she left him, deciding she should keep the final pregnancy intact. She did this at a Catholic home for unwed mothers, and helped pay her way by sweeping floors and washing linen. There she delivered, and gave away, a gently wailing girl.

Andrea found a new apartment in another city, and painted every room, and as soon as her breasts and womb quit trickling, started a new job. Very often she walked the two miles to work. And some nights she walked home again across the bridge and down bright streets. It was by far the easiest thing she'd ever done, bringing in generous tips serving drinks in the shadowy lounge of an over-priced seafood restaurant, the tables heavily varnished over pirate maps, black beams fastened with ropes and nets and fake ships' wheels.

This is what she had deliberately left behind her: *being shown, being told, being made to.* Although she shopped for serious discounts, her shoes were now Italian and all of her clothes bore good labels.

In this leaving behind of things, there was never a thought of abandoning men altogether, for she had always drawn them without any effort, and she enjoyed them. But she now understood exactly where her talents lay, and that just one talent was safe to develop recklessly.

As for men, they were becoming Andrea's men, and they existed in the lounge. They came in after work, generally in suits and ties; they came in after dinners or meetings or for the evening itself; they often came in because Andrea was there, safe and entertaining, sometimes outrageous. She never forgot an order, she never crossed the line no matter how hard one of them might try, and was sweet to any woman who might be with them. They saw her in the ways they wanted to, sometimes in ways that would have shaken her badly if she'd known.

For Andrea, the world had finally become a place which she believed she not only understood, but had a part in building.

The girls she worked with also liked to dress well and have fun, and if they were slightly in awe of Andrea, she only felt it her due, and took the best care of them she could. She worried with them over their boyfriend troubles or mothers who phoned too often, and brought little presents to share, sushi or interesting finds from bakeries around the city. When pressed, she laughed and reminded them she was on the rebound, and the stories she came up with about her old boyfriends were all imagined or altered versions of events with Mark.

During her hours off she bought cookbooks and whisks and separators and special spoons and copper bottomed pans, and spent entire mornings mastering Greek pastry, stuffed artichoke hearts, sauces, fondant.

Very occasionally she would bring someone home at night. Andrea would wake him with eggs benedict and espresso, but if he ever phoned after that, she'd reject him with such grace he rarely tried again. There were two rules. The first was instinctive: she avoided any man with either too much sadness or too much lady-killer about him; he had to seem content before she showed interest. The second was conscious, and greatly lessened her choices — he could not live in that city, he had to come from somewhere else.

To celebrate her twenty-first birthday, she set up a party in the small private dining room of an Italian restaurant. She traded hours with the owner to help pay for it.

To make a lucky thirteen she invited twelve men, her favourite customers, and there was a lot of teasing over her celebrating a birthday she must have seen a few times before. She didn't correct them. They all showed up, some with wives or lovers. Andrea had learned how to throw a good time; they downed orange martinis and wine and crusty breads, salmon antipasto and tiny crab cakes until eleven thirty, the end, as stated on her invitation.

She said goodbye to a few hopeful stragglers and left in a cab, her arms heaped with bath oils, Spanish champagne, jokey cards and single red roses.

She kicked off her heels and, a bit drunkenly, sliced the ends from the roses and set each into a slender green olive oil bottle.

Then she washed out the fridge.

That night she dreamed she wore a soft blue beret and a very conservative powder blue suit. She was going to the Lady Chapel. But couldn't recall the rosary or the One Saint who should be there for her.

It wasn't surprising to her even in the dream, this confusion. God was all for polished wood and everybody kneeling, Christmas and Easter, praying for their sins. Sin was a word that had a comforting old-fashioned ring to it. Sin was the act of taking a blade to the firm skin of a lemon. When the lemon was scraped clean it was sin that did it, and left the zest as a result.

But still, when she woke, there remained an almost sweet ache for something she hadn't been able to bring to mind in the dream.

One night she lifted her long skirt to just above the knees. She had just served four of her regulars. They were drinking, to the man, scotch: neat, with water, water on the side, soda. On one leg she'd written with ballpoint pen, in thick letters, *salt*. On the other, pepper (but the "r" was reversed because she'd written upside-down and back-wards that day).

Salt and pepper shakers. She said it serious, dropped the skirt so fast she knew nobody else had seen it and walked calmly to another table, leaving the men with choked, admiring laughter.

When she returned to them her look was all business. Smiling but business.

How are your drinks, can I get you anything from the kitchen? She glanced to the bar, set a clean ashtray on the old, picked them both up, and left the dirty one on her tray.

All four of them leaned away from her, grinning wisely as if, she thought, they were expecting an encore.

So do we get an encore?

She pretended to blink surprise at the one who'd voiced it. *Pardon?*

The salt and pepper shakers.

They're on the table, Sir.

That cracked them up. And she could hear them laugh again when she came back with a plate of calamari for the couple by the door.

That "r" bothered her. If a tattoo artist had done it, the words would have been perfect.

It had taken her forever, bending awkward and naked, the mirror imaging her long thighs and a slightly puckered belly with its still unfamiliar fold. Even with the real shakers beside her to copy the lettering, she'd got it wrong; but you just can't easily erase ballpoint pen from skin. It had to wear for a while. But what was the option? And of course the joke wouldn't last as long as a tattoo. Years and years from now she might be on the beach, in Cozumel for instance. Shades and Bermuda shorts. And some kid would say Mom I just saw something written on that lady's wrinkly chicken skin legs.

Two in the morning she grated carrots into a batter made from fresh eggs, raisins, butter and unbleached organic flour. She cleaned the bathroom until the timer went off, then sipped cocoa for ten minutes. Released the cake from its springform, and slept.

The cake wasn't for her. She ate very little of what she made, but tasted as she cooked and sometimes fed company, usually a waitress with boyfriend.

Next morning she made a cream cheese icing and delivered the cake to the bartender's sister, who'd complained to her of the store-bought flavour of a six-buck slice of congo pie but also said what the hell she herself couldn't bake.

One Sunday evening Andrea had just peeled shallots. Pastry, made the day before, was wrapped in damp cloth, the chives were already snipped and new potatoes scrubbed. In her hand the chef's knife moved easily on the cutting board until the bulbs were minced, faintly purple-red, and fragrant. She straightened, to stretch her back, then stood very still. There might have been a hollow knock, like a single echo of the dull chop on wood.

For a moment that one small noise paralyzed her. She looked toward the door.

Even as she became aware of her lack of makeup, and of the full apron folded from the top and tied around her waist — ideas appeared in ways not possible when she'd last seen him. Mark pies and loaves and stock, Mark tortellini, patés and infusions. She knew how to make this come about. If she had told him to close his eyes and turn around he'd have done it for a game, and let her slide the knife up into the base of his skull. It would have felt like cutting air; he had no substance.

These were not angry visions, but they woke her up a little and she'd needed to rid herself of that terrible heaviness.

Or she could invite him in. She was alone. The computer guy had left that morning after drawing her a little map to show the province in India where his family came from; the sheets were changed and there was fresh orange juice. But she would have to devise a way to get him out again.

Or, she could say *I'm really busy.*

She listened at the door, then opened it to an empty hallway.

Andrea believed she hadn't thought of Mark, not really thought of him, once, after she'd left. When she shared stories at work, his character had entered as a phantom she could easily make disappear. What would he have said to her if he had even made the effort to find her, and then bothered to knock at the door. Nothing. Less than nothing.

She could not and would never again recall his face or his voice.

She had nothing for him. He would know that; he would never come around. She closed the door and got back to work, smiling over a scent which lingered from last night.

REQUIEM

I QUIT.

I hardly ever want a cigarette any more. Next tragedy, I'll do something worthier. Get shitfaced drunk.

He went to Japan and there he stayed.

I lament the passing of my Camel plain ends, no longer beside me in their perfect American soft pack. I used to smoke them one after another, sipping orange juice, or sometimes saki to commemorate his trip without me. Sometimes I still work until morning at the crooked table I rescued from his parents' basement, and painted deep blue enamel.

A little package hovers on the blue surface, a paper box decorated with Japanese postage, a customs sticker stating the amount in Yen, stamped in an alien script, so beautiful. It could say "this way to the ladies' room" and it would still be perfect: pictographs, ink-blocked. A treasure. To become the heart of a series of paintings, like the Impressionists' discovery of silkscreen prints crumpled within imported tea crates. The slim box contains the paintbrush he sent me, and a note in his careful hand, almost an architect's printing: *Russian sable*. Russia so close to Japan. Maybe it was ancestors of the Japanese who gave him an oriental lid, the Slavic eye.

I'm trying to persuade myself that I married him for the challenge, a gauntlet thrown, a classic match; study the opponent, feint and counter, attack and retreat over and over again. Of course, later on it was a brawl.

Nobody believed he would ever submit like he did, commit to one woman. When we went out together I could see the incredulous looks from his friends, their unmasked curiosity: what did she do, what could he possibly see in her. Women phoned him. I smiled, listening to the volume of surprise when he said he was married now, their voices floating across the room to me in tinny crescendos.

Who could ever thaw him, that man of prodigious talent, cool grey eyes, extreme reserve. I was so stupid. I thought he was trying to mask shyness and pain, that he was hurt, and I would fix it, be his protector. I approached him carefully, devised a strategy of cold and heat.

A friend showed him to me first. She assured me he wasn't into sex, so I imagined him as a eunuch, a pitiful castrato to whose heart I would appeal. As it turned out, he just wasn't interested in my friend, or her fair-skinned voluptuousness.

You bet he was into sex. Immediately.

It was like making out with Sir Galahad — what would you like, Lady, what can I do for you? He was an erotic dream come true. I got tired of it. At the end I wanted to say: Be a man. Grab me when I don't want it, hold my wrists and bang the hell out of me. He'd never do that. He liked to make me nuts, half crazy fainting.

What else can I say. I was barely twenty years old and his ego was bigger than the both of us.

I strip for my bath wondering why these men like me; I look almost like a boy, all scruffy haired. I dress like a dyke: workboots, jeans, men's shirts, usually no underwear at all. I can't cook. Why do they even like me. My teeth are crooked.

I had a boyfriend for a while who always brought me flowers, a dutch bunch. Lying beneath him once, I told myself, memorize this instant — this is exquisite and may never happen again. I told myself: I am young, and intend to be young for a while, but don't be fooled, when I'm older, guys will look different. Memorize this instant: he is leaning over you, arms propped straight, his eyes are clear, his skin is lovely and sweet, his beard is trimmed and soft. He is laughing and his teeth are white. He is looking straight into your eyes, his head is cocked slightly and brows arched, asking a laughing silent question — do you feel like I do? He's pleased as hell because I feel so good to him, he tells me so, enters me, gasps and smiles. He is beautiful. And a young man.

So I memorized the moment, dutifully. How I made a young man happy. But especially, how he looked at me so I would know it.

That was very nice of him.

Sometimes they bury their heads in the side of my neck, or the pillow, and they push and moan and I feel like their illusion.

I think my boy with the flowers quit coming over because of the tea kettle. We fell asleep. And the bottom burned right off, so we woke from our nightmares to choking thick smoke of aluminum. Metal burning up in my little kitchen. Almost a fire. A portent.

And if the man I once married comes back from the Orient, where will he sleep?

He has sent me a silk scarf for my birthday, dark moss green with white lilies. He is oblivious to these kinds of things, and wouldn't know lilies are the flowers of the dead.

I am now certain he won't come back to me. Ever.

He had a plan for everything, how we would have grand-children, the design of our wonderful house, the places we'd visit, who would visit us, how I would learn to dress, who we would become. He planned my future, I who'd carefully played him like a trout and took him triumphantly home in my basket. I became fish food.

Don't wish for what you want, you might get it.

I hate that story, those puerile sentiments. Then we are left wishing for everything that's good for our character, dreary and fine and noble and hardworking, that has the appearance of not being over brilliant or unusual, and won't make the gods jealous. Or our neighbours.

Spinning in my apartment, lungs full of American smoke, Albert King on the turntable while I painted, Nina Simone when I needed to feel tough, freeway noise and a milky way of streetlights, Edith Piaf when I wanted to make love like I imagined a French woman would.

Fish food even so.

Any human, entering an ocean and thinking he has control over his boat or his swimming lessons or scuba gear, is reduced to potential food, at the mercy of currents and storms, mechanical accident.

White lilies appear in strange places.

I take to reading Agatha Christie.

I am intrigued by Poirot's infusions, Miss Marple's neighbours; I imagine England as narrow streets and gardeners tending potted roses arranged on flagstone terraces. I read while I stir-fry rice and vegetables on the stove, while I soak in the bath, when I am alone at night, which is almost always. I read quickly, carelessly, hardly ever guessing who done it. Nice neat murders. But I don't really consider murder as an option.

I read between the lines of his cool romantic letters, how he has met a Japanese artist (but doesn't tell me how he played her body like a samisen), how he stayed at the house of a woman who modelled for British *Vogue* (but not saying what she wore for him). They must like him, these oriental women, his detached attentions and confident voice, a man who doesn't growl. I don't know why he writes to me, he never wishes I was there, but can't leave me alone, and says he wants to see me happy. I think he wants me to see him happy, and suffer for it.

But I'd caught him fair and square and he was crazy about me.

I think he had built up a mythology about me and how I would influence his life, as if he'd found a specimen, the young of a fabulous creature. He would talk about my potential. Potential meant I didn't yet fully exist.

Imaginary me.

I have read a few articles about him, seen his work on the lustrous pages of art journals, and sometimes I hear my words in his quotes. I should have copyrighted my mouth, or kept it shut for the years we lived together as wife and man. He has no shame. He still feeds off me.

Sometimes I feel like I'm choking. I can't breathe. I feel my throat for lumps, sit straighter to take pressure off my respiratory plumbing, open windows to the freeway's torment of ice fog and square tires. My pulse feels weak and erratic and I wonder who will find my body. The pipes in the bathroom hiss all night long, and a bat comes out of hibernation into the porch off my kitchen, and I can't decide what colour to paint the hall.

He would have caught the bat and told me what paint to buy and complained to the landlord about the pipes. What am I saying — he would never have lived here.

I had to phone a bass player to get the bat.

I made him tea, and we kept the little bat in a pail until it could be taken outside when he left. I was almost sorry to let that bat go, even though it had frightened me; it had red-gold fur and big ears and wings of brown leather with little clawed hands on the tips.

A WONDERFUL DANCER

MY MOTHER, ELENA, MET RUSSELL AT A BALLROOM DANCE
CLASS. She had come home that first evening and immediately phoned to tell me all about him, this charming
older man who was such a fantastic dancer, and how almost
old-fashioned and awkward he was with her during the
break. I imagined him confidently buzzing my mother
backwards around and around the floor, his age-spotted
hand resting lightly on her back. He would be hunched
in the shoulders, wear a fedora and fat gold rings, and
maybe, later on, spill coffee all over his shoes as he rose to
offer her his chair.

Elena got a kick out of the idea of any man who could
dance like that taking classes just to meet women.

"It worked, though, didn't it," I said.

A few weeks later she said, "He reminds me something
of Bob Hope, you know, the hapless charmer, and he
laughs a lot. But between us, I wonder whether he's a bit
deaf and laughs in the event he thinks he's missed
something and can't make an intelligent response. Now if
you happen to meet him, Clarice, I need to warn you. He
does wear those hats you hate so much. But I think a man

of his age and with the kind of money he's got is entitled to wear any hat he wants."

I first wondered *what* kind of money, and then erased the fedora from my mental picture of Russell. As for Russell's age, apparently he had at least a decade on my mother, who was approaching her mid-sixties when she took up ballroom dancing and discovered him.

She was beautiful, my mother, I'd always thought she was, and she had a sweet kind of vanity which she was very aware of and tried to disguise. Glasses, for instance. She needed them for almost everything, but around guests she'd tuck them away, claiming they were "just for reading", and then myopically pour everyone drinks and serve the meal. Foam pads for her bras. "*Everybody* used to have them," she'd tell me.

She tried to talk me into getting something for my small chest — a bit of padding, Dear, just a little enhancement. It was no use, of course, any more than had been her lectures on permanent waves or my getting rid of leg and pit hair when I was going through a phase in high school. She'd been a student in the Fifties, when girls really did have hideous glasses and their chests were supposed to look like twin launch pads for sweater-loaded missiles. It must have been painful for her to witness my fashion sensibilities. When I was fifteen she started planning, while trying to involve me, the first in a series of versions of my wedding day, hoping against hope that I would eventually succumb to a world of lace and trousseaus and proper foundations. I loved my mother more than anything.

But what to make of Russell? Elena had dated several men younger than herself until she hit sixty, and then, after a couple of fallow years man-wise, she told me she believed her chances of ever meeting Mr. Right were pretty much done. It was a frightening time for her, I knew that. We had lived on money from my father's estate, an investment-based income that kept my mother struggling and sometimes on the verge of having to get a real job. My father was always her *estranged-ex*. How estrange he was for the time, I only discovered in my teens. When I was three, he'd left her for another man. This was the reason, I think, for Elena being what she was, the ultimate sweet and hard-working man-pleaser who needed to know she was woman enough for at least *some* of them out there.

Hence the ballroom dance classes to brush off the rust.

Hence the huge worry over Clarice's dress-sense.

Before I was born, my parents bought a little farm, an acreage really, close to the city. It came with a fairly solid three-storey house, and a slightly tilted barn on a stone foundation. Elena had a sign made for the end of the lane: *Chez Nous Bien Venue*. Elena wanted peacocks, a donkey, a duck pond, chickens for eggs and, when she had children, a couple of ponies. She also had vague plans to make money from doing all of this. My father was an optometrist and couldn't build a henhouse to save his life. He left and *Chez Nous Bien Venue* eventually became a bed and breakfast. This was where I grew up. Although our closest neighbours all thought it was funny to pronounce it *Shays News*, they still referred travellers or visitors to us. Elena met some of her favourite men that way, a few of whom stayed and helped to build things. By the time I was ten, I had learned to drive a nail and paint walls.

About two months into Elena's new courtship, I finally drove out to *Chez Nous* to meet Russell. The sign in the lane was freshly painted, an event which over the years had often signalled love in my mother's life, and I smiled as I wondered which of them had done the work. The winding road to the house, once a rutted and bogged-out car snagger, was graded and gravelled, and the scrawny poplars on either side had grown thick as a birch forest. Parked in front of the house was a maroon Cadillac Seville, very new.

How to describe Russell, and remember exactly how he looked at our introduction? There at my mother's huge, comfortable kitchen table sat a rather handsome older man (I say older because of course I'd expected someone bent and tottery, with maybe frustrated beads of lecherous sweat on his upper lip), a thick-necked, big in the chest, very fit, gentlemanly man. He wore a suit, well-cut but casual, a silver western-style string tie and, *put me out of my misery*, one of those awful cloth and mesh caps that businesses give away to customers. He stood up to shake my hand, just at the same time Elena was taking a tray of hors d'oeuvres from the oven.

I don't know what made me say it to him, but I did. "The second the food hits this table, that hat has got to go."

There was a cavernous second of silence. Then Russell did the right thing; he laughed and took off the cap.

"You are exactly the way how I pictured you," he said. My mother smiled.

At this point, in spite of his syntax, I suddenly worried about what I was wearing, which I remember was something I considered to be slightly dressy — a short cardigan over a long, embroidered Indian silk-blend shirt over leggings and heavy ankle-high boots. Was it all at least ten years too young for me? This ability to achieve two effects from one tiny statement, the first portraying himself

to me as gracious, self-effacing, even forgiving of my rude-
ness, and the second taking the rug out from under me —
this is how I identified Russell as a ladies' man. A ladies'
man knows how to have his way and still keep the lady
happy. He had his little hat revenge all right.

It became clear enough over the next while that Russell
wasn't quite like any of my mother's previous men. She'd
always had a good take on a man's character; it seemed
she could smell a potential creep real fast, and when I was
a kid had warned me away from a couple of our paying
guests. The other men-friends, all younger than herself,
had made Elena look even younger because they adored
her and love makes a person shake off lines and worries
and grants them a certain radiance. But beside Russell,
Elena *was* young, and the few times I was around he babied
and teased her. She called him a cradle robber.

I'm not certain what Russell made of me, but we seemed
to have come to an understanding that Elena was the
important element in our equation, and we were
cautiously polite with each other.

One September weekend I drove out, and as I turned
the last bend into the yard I saw something different at the
entrance to Elena's garden. There was an ornate
mahogany-stained trellis, not the usual store-bought
latticed structure but one, as I discovered, which had a
decorative framework of curlicues, vines and leaves, and
cut into the arch above one's head going into the garden,
several small stars and a medieval kind of sun with flames
like the arms of starfish. It looked as if it had stood there
for years. I knew that it had all been put together, fret-sawn,
sanded and stained by old Russell.

I walked into the kitchen. He was there, as usual, at the table and watching my mother with what I then decided was a great deal of love. I looked at him, maybe it was only for a second, but long enough to be sure that he of the Cadillac had really been capable of building that trellis. I took in the thick old fingers, the broad chest that gave a sense of what once had been great strength, his awful cap sitting meekly on the counter, his carefully polished leather shoes. And he turned around, with regret, I thought, at having to take his eyes off my mother, to give me a nod and smile.

"That is completely gorgeous, Russell."

"He made it for me, Clarice, I bet you thought he just went out and bought it at a garden shop, but this man is an artist." My mother's voice was high and almost silly in her delight.

"She knows I built it, Elena. Don't you Dear?"

Dear was new.

"Figured you had. Although Mom never mentioned you possessed any particular talents aside from foxtrotting and eating outrageous amounts of her cooking."

He squinted at me over that one. "Thought I heard the word 'gorgeous' come out of your mouth a minute ago."

"It is, Russell, it is solid and elegant and imaginative, and by far the prettiest trellis ever to grace any garden I've ever seen. And I loved the grape leaves and stars."

He turned to my mother. "And that's by far the longest compliment I've ever heard about anything from this little girl, here. Is she on something?"

I successfully fought an urge to hug him. For some reason I didn't mind, being in my thirties, being referred to as "this little girl"; it made perfect sense from a guy who agreed he was robbing my mother from her cradle.

Over dinner at Chez Nous that autumn evening, I discovered there were a couple more surprises to Russell. I knew he'd married into a big farming operation and was widowed some years ago, but for the first time, at least in my presence, he talked about his money, which from the sounds of it meant at least a couple of million. "I don't know about what to do with the stuff," he said, "after a point where the bills are paid, food's in the cupboard and you got a little holiday cash set aside, then what you got left is a big stack of funny money. I can't stand dealing with it. My daughter, on the other hand, she's the one with the head for it. Loves all the stocks and banks and playing around. Leave all that nonsense to her, long as my charities are looked after I don't care what she does. She's the smart one." From the way he said it, I believed he didn't really admire that sort of smart.

I admit having inherited some of my mother's aversion to real jobs (although it didn't stop me from taking them), and there was a tiny fantasy right then about Russell giving me a chunk of his funny money and setting me up for life. But the real surprise was a lot more fun. He went out to the Cadillac and returned with a small wooden chest, buffed and scarred, which I knew at once he had made himself. Inside, laid on green felt, and some wrapped in cloth, were tools. His tools, but not those of a carpenter.

"Kept these. Lots of times I wondered why I'd bother, most likely as out of date now as me, but these are the tools of my trade as a young man. These are the hammers, here's mutes, tips, this here's one of the forks." This he rolled out from a wrap of soft yellow cloth. "Two bits to the first one who guesses my trade."

Elena tilted her head and frowned, and said, "A fork? But that looks like something you'd see in the old doctor's office."

"Tuning fork. You were a piano tuner." I am so smug when I know I'm right.

He fished in his pocket for a quarter, and I accepted it.

"Used to rebuild them sometimes, too. Not much time for that and not much call for it out there." He motioned east, where miles and miles from *Chez Nous* or any place else he had once learned to be a farmer. Then he poked my arm and said, "Ha. I knew you'd be impressed."

I was, but exactly why he thought I would be I'm not sure. I guess that's when I began to almost love Russell myself.

I had now come across two piano tuners in my life although I've never owned a piano, and both of these were in fact former piano tuners.

When I was nineteen I met a guy on the train I was taking to Vancouver. He was quite a bit older, maybe late twenties, and during the ride we had some fun, spooky talks which included the concept of *now*. We decided there is no now, now is always gone. By the time you're aware of now, it's old news. We came to other conclusions about the slippery reality of Time, and laughed when we decided it was useless to think about. Now I know what a rare and privileged thing it is to meet any human being anywhere and begin talking in the way we did. He laughed at my name, Clarice, for being old-fashioned and something that Walt Disney would have named an early cartoon cow. I thought I would never forget that guy, but almost twenty years later his face is long gone and I am unable to say for certain what his name was. It may have been Toby.

It was Toby who told me about Pythagoras, a word I'd only heard in high-school geometry. This is pretty much what he'd told me, although I looked it up again:

In the 6th century BC, Pythagoras taught that the heavenly bodies moved from west to east, and that each of them moved at a rate proportionate to its distance from the central fire. This fire is the Hearth of the Universe.

The ten heavenly bodies include the firmament of the fixed stars, the five planets, the sun, the moon, the earth, and the counter-earth. The counter-earth is the body under the earth which moves parallel with it and at the same rate, and therefore is invisible. The counter-earth is nearest to the Hearth Fire, and it hides the Fire from earth, so we may never look directly into the face of God.

The harmonic movements of these bodies produce a great song, the Music of the Spheres. This is the music which Moses heard on the Mount, and which we will all hear at the time of our death.

Pythagoras also made the discovery that if two strings have the same degree of tension, but one is half the length of the other, then when they are plucked the pitch of the short string is exactly one octave higher than the other. This last bit was given to me along with far more information than I ever want to hear again concerning definitions of musical scales, harmonics and so on. The reason Toby knew so much was that he had been a piano tuner. He'd been making a pretty good living at it but what he really wanted was to compose, and sing in a rock band. For the past year he'd been redefining himself and getting ready to make the leap to become an artist. *When I get off this train,* he'd told me, *the wolves will be waiting.*

He took such pleasure in talking about the Music of the Spheres, in spite of calling it nonsense revived for aristocrats in the Middle Ages.

I still think it was a wonderful way for them to order the cosmos, with no worries over confusing ideas like infinity, knowing we all exist securely within lawful boundaries placed on the universe; and meanwhile all the heavenly bodies are singing away beneath the fixed — and also singing — dome of stars. But of all of the heavenly bodies I especially loved that veiled planet beneath our own.

I sometimes thought I might be able to feel it if I stood very still and very relaxed, if I spaced my feet exactly in the right way, and parallel to one another. I thought I might be able to feel the counter-earth spinning and ponderous in its heavy, invisible orbit beneath me, always on the other, the shadowed side of the earth. The counter-earth would not be cold, I thought, although maybe it ought to be. It would be very, very warm, and possibly humid. Its natural inhabitants would seem unnatural to us and they had no names, both because they had never been seen by a living human, and had never been suspected of existing. Its natural flora would be pale and succulent and also forever nameless. This is what the counter-earth did: it breathed dreams into the sleeping minds of humans, and into the minds of those who are lost in deep thought, and as it spun its slow rotation, it gathered those dreams back again. The earth and the counter-earth, two globes, each unaware of the other, mixing up the ingredients of dreams as they spun together; and the sighing of the invisible wind created between them was one of the notes that made the generative music heard sometimes in dreams, and at the moment of our death.

I now wonder whether Toby, or whoever he was, had managed to leave only the piano tuner behind for the wolves to devour and had kept his composer self leaping ahead.

I now wonder how badly Elena wanted to marry Russell.

Russell became a fixture at *Chez Nous*. He didn't exactly move in, but most times I visited, it was evident he'd been spending nights there. Over the following summer, when Elena kept the occasional paying guest, Russell very properly had a separate room as if he, too, were just passing by. He worked for his board. The sign at the lane was given a frame and new legs, furniture was tightened up and revarnished; he was always in search of something that needed fixing or a coat of paint. He started to call my mother his child bride.

For all the money he had, Russell was never extravagant with Elena. I think she would have enjoyed something over the top, maybe good jewellery or a nice car, a real vacation.

We were all talking one time, about where we'd each most love to travel. Elena said she longed, most winters, for hot sun and ocean, maybe Mexico for a month. I voted for Italy and the south of France. Russell had been the quietest. Then he stood, and said, "Don't you know, I always thought about Scotland. Two grandparents and some cousins came from there someplace, think my daughter's wrote it down, but I think it's about time I gave it some serious thought."

We all got pretty excited over this. Russell was talking himself deeper into it and helping my mother decide the best time of year to leave the place and who'd look after it and for how long. I volunteered to research travel arrangements and accommodation for them.

It never happened. There seemed to be good reasons but I don't remember what they were, except the understanding was they only meant a postponement, a delay in plans.

My mother had always spoken with me about many kinds of things, but she was careful never to intrude with much of her intimate life. She believed that men were, by nature, transient. Even so, more and more I could see the disappointment in the set of her mouth, in deepened creases around her eyes, in the slowing of her steps around the house at Chez Nous.

One night at dinner Russell finally noticed it too. Elena got up to clear the dishes and Russell suddenly reached out and held her hand between both of his. "Don't be sad, don't be sad," he said. "What is it?"

He had asked the worst possible question. Elena began to sob, terrible harsh sobs that had us on our feet and almost fighting over who should hold my mother while she cried away what I knew was all the sadness of a lifetime. The sadness over never again having a young man in her bed, over all her other children who never were, and over her only husband who left on a trip one day and never came home. We both embraced her, which meant somewhat uncomfortably having to embrace each other, and all the while Russell softly chanted, "What is it? What is it?"

I don't know how long we stood like that.

We finally broke apart, and as I left to get my mother another handkerchief I willed Russell to do the right thing while they were alone, to say the right thing. I thought he had. When I came into the kitchen he was whispering to her, "Anything. Anything you want. I promise."

She began to cry again, and then she said, "I always wanted chickens."

Sweet person that I am, I started to laugh. But so did my mother.

Russell seemed a little bewildered by both the chickens and the sudden change in weather, but he braved it out. He immediately offered a henhouse and the birds to fill it, and Elena and I laughed harder. Then she gave him a big laugh-shaken kiss on the mouth.

I still had faith in Russell's promise, I believed he would either keep offering it, or would understand that for Elena to have both a man and chickens at the same time, meant that the man was there to stay.

Not long after the time of Elena's show of sorrow, Russell himself began to slow down in certain ways. What I'd first read in him as being the relaxed state of a contented man, now appeared to be more like those long, inward-seeing sessions that some of the old occupy their days with. He had truly wanted to build that henhouse, but we all decided it would be just the same if he hired the job out, and next spring that's what he did. Elena had really only dreamed of having a few pretty hens around for colour and clucking and eggs. But Russell ordered fifty sexed Cornish cross chicks, the minimum the hatchery would sell, had a neighbour deliver straw for the bedding, and showed up one day with heat lamps, feeders, chick starter, cardboard for fencing, and what looked like a dress box — a jumpy, cheeping dress box.

My mother phoned me daily with chick reports. She was an early morning person and discovered she and fifty tiny birds had lots in common; she loved feeding them and they loved it too. Every day she picked up each one and spoke with it, and encouraged the shy ones to the water dish after discouraging the pushy ones away. After two weeks, she hadn't lost a single chick. Russell couldn't get over it, he'd warned her to expect up to a dozen that first week, and told me he'd best start calling her the gee-dee *Saint* Elena. The chicks quickly lost their yellow down and sprouted weird, uneven white feathers, and went through voice changes and soon we suspected that some of them were female impersonators.

The third weekend in May of that year hit a record cold spell. I am not clear on exactly what happened the night I got the first call from Russell, whether he had checked the temperature in the henhouse first, or exactly why he phoned to tell me about it, but he said Elena had woken up and was worried about the birds.

My phone rang again, just past four in the morning. Russell's voice, but a slurred, almost zombie-ish voice. "It's all burned. Everything. It's all gone. You better come."

That was not even the worst of all the worst moments. I believed that *Chez Nous Bien Venue* was in ashes, my mother's beautifully kept house, the crooked barn, the trellis and garden, the poplars, all. And where was Elena, what was keeping her warm? I don't know how I managed to speak then, let alone make the drive to the country.

"Where is she, where's my mother?"

"In the kitchen, here. You better come."

I could hear someone talking, a man's voice, and then that voice came on the phone.

"This Clarice? It's Ed Morris, down the road."

"What does he mean, Mom's in the kitchen?" I hated how I sounded, all strangled and screechy.

"Everything's fine, Russell had the sense to call me. You just calm down. It's the chickens are gone, all burnt up, and the house. A couple other guys have been here and left already, it was a fast burn and nothing spread."

"The henhouse."

"The henhouse. I guess old Russell here got out of bed, it was so cold middle of the night, and seems he plugged in an extra light for the birds to keep them warm. Sounds like a short. Your Mom's had an upset, though."

My mother was not in the kitchen when I got out there, but lying on the couch, white as white. Someone had covered her in quilts and made her tea, which was untouched.

Russell had pulled up a chair beside her. He seemed to me then, a very old man.

I spoke so softly to my mother, I touched her face and embraced her so gently because I was afraid she had already died. She put her arms around me, but there was so little force in her, they lay across my back. She said, "I don't feel well, Clarice."

Russell cried as I phoned the ambulance. And as we waited, he took my hands and gripped so hard it hurt. "Forgive me. Please don't hate me."

"Don't be silly, I don't hate you Russell." I thought it was a weird thing for him to say to me.

But my mother, a much younger woman than she should have been, died that afternoon.

Russell, who had already aged so suddenly, responded to his deep loss by gradually shedding thin layers of himself and not replacing them.

It was some months before I had the heart to finally empty *Chez Nous* and put the property up for sale. By then, Russell had sold his little house in the city, and moved into an apartment complex which gave him meals and nursing care if needed. At first, my visits with him were more for myself, to grieve, and I would talk and laugh with him about my beautiful mother, believing Russell still had strength to share. After a while I stopped by only every couple of weeks. By then, the conversation was mostly myself talking and Russell nodding, or occasionally responding with "Don't say. Well now."

A year and a half after Elena died, four years after she fell for Russell's dancing, Russell's nurse phoned to say he'd been moved to hospital, palliative care.

I don't know why I felt obliged to visit the ward of the dying and stay with Russell. He wasn't my family. Maybe I thought Elena would appreciate it since she wasn't there for him, for those final intimate talks and the giving of reassurance.

There would be no talks as such; he was in a deep coma. I couldn't know for certain whether Russell would be aware of me at his side, or could listen, whether he was lonely or in pain, if my presence would soothe him.

I pulled a chair up so I could sit close to his face and I began to say useless things like, *It's okay.* Sometimes his face twitched and his mouth opened into a jerking, angle-jawed kind of grin. His eyes stayed closed. I was with him no more than fifteen minutes when I could hear a woman talking loudly down the hall and heading my way. She strode in

— tall, heavy-breasted, long-footed, middle aged — and very startled to see me.

"Well, Daddy's got some company. And just who are you exactly?"

"Clarice, Elena's daughter." Exactly.

"Oh yes," she said, with way too much volume, "Daddy's friend who died last year. Sorry for your troubles."

She was eyeing my chair.

"Sorry. Here, you should take it, I'll go sit by the window."

"No that's just fine. I flew in from Kingston last night and sat right there for hours. Not a wink of sleep in case he'd wake up and say something. Like what, I'm sure I don't know. So you're Clarice. I thought you'd be younger."

"Pardon?"

"From the way Daddy talked about you, I thought you'd be much younger."

I really didn't want to know what that meant, and gave no response.

"So you're a magazine person or something, I hear."

"An editor, one of them. I work different places." I was trying to be conversational; I thought she needed to take her mind off Russell. She, Russell's daughter, whose name was so seldom mentioned by her father.

"I apologize, but your name has just disappeared on me."

"Magdalen. It's uncommon enough so don't feel bad. So, is it a women's magazine?"

"Cultural, literary."

She sighed loudly. "Well I could tell you some stories, the things I've gone through, I could write a book."

She wandered the room as she talked, picking things up and putting things down, opening her handbag and fishing around and closing it. I wondered if she was hyper-active. If people of that age could be.

"Elena was around Daddy quite a lot, I understand, though we never met. Well, it's a good thing in a way for old people to get together like they seem to these days."

"Actually, Russell was around Mom's place quite a lot." And Elena wasn't old.

"Whatever. Would you be a dear and stay with him, I really need to get a bite."

"Go ahead, I'll be here."

Russell was quiet. Besides an occasional tremor or spasm in his legs, he hadn't moved at all.

I whispered to him, "Hey, I finally met your daughter Magdalen. But you know what Russell, I think she's a case."

He suddenly took a deep, shuddering breath and I almost fell off the chair. I bit my lower lip, ashamed at my big mouth. But maybe he wasn't listening to that, or anything else, or maybe he agreed with me and that's what upset him.

"I'm sorry." I said nothing more, and after a while Magdalen returned.

She didn't say a thing, but stood and stared out the window.

I struggled for conversation. "My mother said Russell was a wonderful dancer."

She glanced at me, then went back to the window view.

"Yes. Daddy said that's how they met. Lots of lonely women out there, lots of them widows and needing the security of a man."

The room had become stuffy and hot. I took off my sweater. "My mother was very independent. She raised me on her own."

"Well good for her. Then she really didn't need Daddy, did she?"

"Well. Yes she did, I think she loved him very much." I was turned sideways in the chair and had one arm on Russell's bed, braced as if I'd been going to jump up. What would I do, what would I do if Magdalen didn't shut up.

Magdalen sat by the window and smiled at me. I'd seen that smile before; it's the same one certain girls at school gave me when they'd just got the higher mark on a test, or the cute boy had talked to them instead of me. "I'm very glad to hear she loved him and they gave each other some joy in later years. As you likely know, Daddy and I were in touch a lot over this relationship. You just never know." She tittered.

I had the sensation I sometimes get when driving alongside a police car. It's a maddening routine of watching my speed carefully and feeling guilty for no reason and wanting to say: it wasn't me officer, I didn't do it. How stupid to even think I had to respond at all to this idiot Magdalen. What the hell was I expected to say, oh gosh no I'm not after your dad's money and neither was Elena, no sir. I really wished Russell in his deathbed coma would sit up right then and yell *Call in the lawyers. I leave everything to Elena's daughter who dresses funny.* That would shut her up.

But Magdalen wouldn't shut up. "As long as everybody knows what's what in terms of family, if you catch my drift. I was always very careful with Daddy and his investments and so on, and stayed in touch with his lawyer. So of course, when he started to arrange pre-nuptials I was alerted."

Russell was not going to sit up and say a thing. Russell had not said a thing while living, not a word to me about marrying my mother, not a word about this woman stopping it. He could easily have overstepped Magdalen, he could have ignored her, he could have asked my advice. Then I understood the trip that never happened, Magdalen talked him out of it and he'd said not a word about that, either. My mother must have known some of this nasty business, how could she not?

Russell, the ladies' man, had asked me not to hate him.

Then I heard it, I swear. A swift swell of music. It was there and then it wasn't. I turned to Magdalen, ready to forgive her in a second, but she was glaring at me.

I reached over and held Russell's arm tight for the encouragement that I needed to look at him. His jaw was relaxed and, for the first time, his eyes were slightly open. He was utterly still.

"Magdalen, your dad is gone."

She shrieked and I moved away from Russell's bed, out of the room and along the hall.

Then I heard it once more — God's music, the Music of the Spheres — and I walked toward the sound, laughing at my silliness; in this ward of the dying of course there would be a music room. It was there I found a lean old guy at the piano, playing softly and alone, playing something gentle and jazzy that I thought I should recognize, maybe a Gershwin tune. On each of his age-spotted hands was a fat gold ring.

I leaned in the doorway, listening until he'd finished; and when the music stopped, he looked my way and bowed slightly.